YOUNG BLOOD

J.E. Taylor

Young Blood © 2022 J.E. Taylor

Cover Art by Eerilyfair Design's Book Cover and Logo Art

YOUNG BLOOD

Duty and fate collide when a cocky young alpha finds his forbidden mate.

Robby Young never anticipated meeting his true soul mate on the first day at the Monster Defense Academy, especially considering relationships with other members of the agency are strictly prohibited.

When that girl ends up listed as his partner, Robby has to muzzle his wolf to keep her safe.

If he falls prey to his desires and crosses the line his father set, he'll sentence his partner to a position in front of the firing squad.

1

AS WE CRESTED THE top of the hill, I caught the first view of my home for the next year. The Monster Defense Academy sprawled out before us, tucked in a valley of the Appalachian Mountains of New York. Dark, squat buildings surrounded the center high-rise that gleamed in the midday sun. The entire footprint of the academy was bigger than most small colleges, but the interconnected buildings made it look like a giant octopus with a huge dick sticking out of its center.

"Do I really have to..." I started, still staring at the buildings with enough disgust that I was sure it bled into my face.

"Yes," my father said from the driver's seat before I could finish my sentence. He glanced at me with the same piercing blue eyes I saw in the mirror on a daily basis. "You're a legacy. You will carry on our tradition. One day, maybe you'll be running the company."

I scoffed. After all the information my father fed me over the years, I didn't want anything to do with the Monster Defense Agency. But my father had grand plans for me, whether I liked it or not. Leading the Allegany pack was one thing, and that I was all for. But walking in his shoes at the MDA? No way. I wanted nothing to do with that.

Unfortunately, I had no goddamn choice.

At least I wouldn't be here alone. The rest of the legacies in the pack would be here with me. We'd be paired with witches and then hunt the vilest creatures out there. That might just be the only thing I looked forward to. Ripping apart vampires had its own sick appeal, especially because a vampire was responsible for the rest of my family's deaths.

The only reason I was breathing today was the fact on that fateful night, I was not home with my mom and my younger brother and sister. I was at my beta's birthday party. Me and a half dozen others watching late-night television, laid out in sleeping bags on the family room floor while a vampire feasted on my family. I still remember my father arriving at Johnson's house before the sun rose the next morning. His eyes had been frantic as he searched the sleeping bags on the floor and when they landed on me, it seemed all that tension turned into something else that made his eyes shine. Relief. Disappointment. I have no idea, but blood streaked his shirt and hands, and he had some in his hair, too.

That night was the only time in my life that I ever recall my father visibly shaken. And dread filled me at the tears shining in his eyes. He took me aside and delivered the news that shattered my world.

I shook the memory away as we pulled up to the grand entrance of the academy. We were the only ones up here on the plateau, looking down at the lower parking lot where the rest of the wolves and witches were being unloaded from buses and cars.

"Why aren't we unloading down there?" I waved to the mass of new recruits.

"We're the elite. This is where I enter."

I hated the superiority in his voice. I glanced at the lower parking lot, wishing I was with them.

A crop of red hair caught my attention and I blinked, with my duffel bag halfway to my shoulder. Even from this distance, I caught her attitude and the ream of swears spilling from her mouth as they hauled her off the bus. Something inside me stirred.

A slap against the back of my head brought me back into the present. "Everyone here is off-limits. You're going to marry the right wolf. You understand?"

"One you deem worthy?" My voice dripped with sarcasm. He was going to marry me off to some alpha's daughter once he found a worthy alliance. It was not my choice. None of this was my choice.

He glared at me.

"Fine. I get it." But my gaze kept drifting to the crowd below. Not only did I wish I was with the rest of my pack, now I wanted to seek out that girl.

"I'm serious. No fucking around here. You keep your nose clean and learn everything you need to do the job right." He shook his finger in my face.

I had to clench my jaw against the urge to bite his digit off. Instead, I hauled the duffel bag over my shoulder and headed inside where a short, bespectacled man led me to my dorm room in silence.

White painted cinderblocks and gray linoleum flooring met my gaze as I stepped into the room the little man waved at. It certainly did not instill any sort of excitement for being here, especially considering the furniture looked too small for my stature. But I guess it was better than sleeping on the hard floor.

A bathroom stood to the right of the entrance door, and the entire thing was about as big as my oversized walk-in shower at home. The scent of antiseptic in the bathroom permeated everything, as if it had just been scrubbed clean. It was enough to sting my nose.

"The assembly starts in twenty minutes in the grand hall." He left me to claim a bed.

I threw my duffel bag on the single bed on the right, assessing the lack of length. Man, if I stretched out on that thing, my lower legs would hang off. I was going to seriously miss my California king at home. I ran my hand over my face, irritated at the prospect of spending a year in this glorified coat closet. I turned and stormed out. I didn't want to be the last person into the assembly, and I wanted to catch that brazen redhead, despite my father's warning.

He wanted me to marry a nice werewolf. Someone subservient. But I liked my women feisty and bold, not meek and mild. And I didn't care what she was. Human, witch, wolf, fae: it didn't matter to me. The only off-limits species was vampire, because those monsters were the walking dead. They even smelled hideous.

I followed my nose, and searching for the assembly hall took less time than I anticipated. It wasn't difficult. I just followed the magical signatures filling the air. Wolves and witches filled the entry leading to the assembly room. Because I had been in the sleeping quarters, I entered the hall on the balcony level and descended the stairs as I scanned the crowd.

Johnson, my beta and the reason I wasn't in a grave with the rest of my family, gave me a wave. I nodded at him but didn't head where he and the rest of my pack stood in a tight circle. My gaze kept moving, past the frown on my father's face, and over the nameless crowd, until it locked with hers.

The reaction was immediate, like a shot to my chest. Her eyes widened as she took me in, and the smile that toyed on her lips had my wolf nearly in a frenzy to claim her. I stepped off the stairs on legs that felt like rubber, and I lost her in the crowd now that I didn't have a clear view.

I cut my way through the mob, catching sight of her as I maneuvered around people. She moved toward me, and when we met in the middle of the gathering, it was as if everyone disappeared. Her chocolate eyes scanned me.

"Hi."

Even her voice made me want to drop to my knees in front of her. Her beauty made the rest of the women in the room seem like hags.

"Hi." I put out my hand. "I'm Robby Young."

"Sarah Stone." She took my hand in a sure grip and pumped once before breaking the contact.

But her touch was enough for me to know.

My father had told me what happens when we meet our true mates. The wolf in me reacted to her, and I had to struggle to keep him in check, despite the crowd surrounding us. He wanted to stake his claim on this wild one right here. I inhaled her citrusy scent as if it were more precious than air. This wasn't just physical, either; it was as if my soul cried out for her, and the glint in her eyes was enough to make me step closer.

A hand landed on my shoulder. I almost didn't turn away from her, but the hand squeezed hard enough to break whatever spell she had on me. I turned, meeting my father's stern gaze.

"The assembly is starting." He didn't remove his hand, either. He pulled me away from Sarah Stone with an iron grip. The scowl on his face screamed disgust, as if my being near her threatened his fucking kingdom.

I glanced over my shoulder and caught the flame of her hair in the crowd as we entered the assembly.

"She is off-limits." His growling voice filled my ear.

I snapped my gaze to his. "What?" I shook his hand off my shoulder. "But she's my true mate." There was no way I was staying away from her.

His step faltered, and his glare homed in on mine. "The MDA will not tolerate interagency relationships."

"It's not like she's my partner." I rolled my eyes at him. "Besides, they made an exception for you and Mom," I pointed out.

Although the agency did have a strict rule against becoming romantically entangled, he and my mother had gotten a pass. I didn't know whether that was because of his legacy standing or because he had become invaluable to the agency, but they didn't crucify either of them. Scolded them, from what I understand, but did not kill them for their transgressions.

Of course, if they had been partners, it would have been a very different story. That's why the agency matched males with males and females with females—it lowered the opportunity for that to happen. The punishment for violating that rule was archaically severe. And not in a job loss way.

It usually meant forfeiting the witch's life, unless they were powerful mages. Then, in that case, the wolf met their end. It was all way too militant for my tastes.

"She was a wolf." He grunted at me, as if that made a difference. "That girl is a witch." He led me up front, where he pointed to the aisle seat before he headed up on stage with the rest of the agency board.

I turned, scanning the auditorium. My gaze landed on her in the back row on the far side of the auditorium. When she looked my way, my lips tilted into a smile. She responded with a grin and a little wave of her fingers.

Man, my wolf was in so much trouble.

I turned back to the stage, to a searing glare from my father. He leaned over to the board members and whispered something I could not pick up. The shock on their faces made me shift in the seat but they nodded at him and took out a bound ledger, marking it up.

When Mr. Simmons, the headmaster of the Monster Defense Academy, stepped up to the podium, the lights dimmed. I stared at the non-descript human as if he wasn't there. I mean, his lips moved and his hands moved in an animated fashion, but I did not hear a word he said.

My mind was focused entirely on the redheaded girl in the back row.

2

A S SOON AS WE were excused from the assembly, I stood to leave.

"Robert," my father called as he hustled down the stairs.

I hated when he called me by my formal name. I was Robby to all my friends and everyone else in the family. I never asked to be a junior, and I tried like hell to differentiate myself. Even with my friends, who were loyal because I treated them with respect and not because I instilled fear in them.

I had the capacity to pull the alpha card and force loyalty, but I never used it. I wasn't into the control game that so many other alphas, my father included, were into.

When Robert Young Senior was out for blood, the pack quaked. He had a mean streak that would make any self-respecting wolf run with their tail tucked between their legs. He ruled the pack through fear, and it irked me. Although, I had to admit that even I got a little skittish when he was on a rampage.

"What?" I snapped. I couldn't wait until he left, and I was free to be myself.

"Remember. Learn." His stern finger waggled at me. "Nothing else. Understand?"

"Yes, sir." Arguing never boded well with my father. And I was still a month shy of eighteen, so technically, he was still in charge of my decisions. At least until he left the campus. Then I was on my own.

"And you will stay away from that girl." He pushed his alpha influence on me.

It draped over me like a wet blanket, chilling me, but I just stared back at him, unwilling to cower, especially on this point.

The muscles in his face jumped, as though he ground his teeth. While other wolves in the vicinity nearly folded in on themselves or turned and hurried along to get away from this display of power that my father was attempting to wield over me, it didn't faze me.

I didn't accept his authority on this one.

"Damn it, boy. Do you want to ruin your life?"

"No, sir." I didn't have a choice in the path he set me on. It was expected of the pack to serve up their young to this organization like sacrificial lambs. As such, I wasn't necessarily going to play by their rules of engagement, especially because my wolf demanded I claim that girl, and who was I to ignore my wolf?

"Then do as I demand," he growled, low.

I neither nodded nor shook my head, but I did turn and walk away, leaving him to stew at my non-reaction. I headed straight to my room, like we had been instructed, to unpack before dinner. Then after we ate, we were expected to head back to our rooms for the night.

My father arranged for Johnson to be my roommate. Allegany pack members usually had pre-arranged roommates who were part of the pack, but from what I understood, they usually opted to room with their partners. Even so, I was glad Johnson was my roommate and not some stranger. It was an indication at how fundamentally powerful the pack was to the MDA.

When I got to my room, it was still empty. Johnson hadn't had a chance to bring his stuff to the room like I had as the son of the grand master of the entire Northeast region. By the time I had unpacked my duffel bag, Johnson strolled in with an expression I recognized.

My father had gotten to him.

He threw his bag on the other bed and turned, opening his mouth.

"Don't." I put my hand up. "I do not want to hear whatever the hell he told you to say."

Rick Johnson closed his mouth and ran his hand through his dark hair. "Okay, man, but it's your funeral."

"My dad got them to change the rules. I can, too." It was cocky to think that way, and I knew it, but there was no way on God's green earth that I was going to deny my wolf this.

"Maybe I'll sleep with her."

Before he even finished saying the thought, I had him against the wall. The growl that tore from me was enough to make Johnson wide-eyed. "If you want to see the sunrise, I suggest you kill that urge right now."

"Shit. Fine." He put his hands out, palms forward in submission. "I didn't realize..." He trailed off, eyes still wide with shock.

"She's my true mate, and I'm not letting my father, or the MDA, dictate what I can and cannot do with her."

"Robby, they are serious with their rules. Besides, you don't know if she's into you. She's not a wolf. She wouldn't feel the connection you're feeling."

I nodded, stepping away from him. Her pupils had dilated when we first met, as I'm sure mine had. But did that mean she was into me? I didn't know, but I sure as hell was going to find out.

I spun away from Johnson and stalked out of the room in search of the dining hall in this monstrous academy. When I finally found the dining room, it was still locked, so, I parked my ass on one of the benches in the hallway, waiting. Not for the doors to open, but for my redheaded dream to walk by.

The door to the opposite hallway creaked, and I caught a glimpse of red hair poke through. I had to clamp down on the smile. She liked being first, too. Either that or she was on the same mission I was.

"This is the dining hall." I allowed a small smile at her gasp, and then her wide eyes landed on me.

"Why are you so early?" She looked around at the deserted hallway.

"I'm hungry." I shrugged. "And I hate to wait in line."

She slid into the spot next to me. "I like to be early so the food isn't picked over too much." She stretched her legs out and crossed her ankles and arms, leaning against the wall with the kind of smile on her face that stirred more than my wolf. Her hair was long, with the kind of waves you see on the beach in the summer, but not frizzy, and the color wasn't the scream-in-your-face red that you get with dye. I had seen too many girls back home try to achieve this look, and it always turned out unnatural. Sarah's hair was a subtle auburn that truly turned heads.

My wolf demanded that I claim her right now, but I couldn't just get down to business right here in the hallway, despite how much I wanted to. Plus, I still didn't know whether she was into me or not, and claiming someone who wasn't on the same page was unthinkable. At least in my world it was, but I've seen it happen and the claimed were always resentful. I didn't want to start a life with anyone based on resentment.

"So, are you here by choice or was this forced upon you, too?" She stared at the doors that led to the dining hall.

"It's expected of me." I sighed.

She snorted. "So, you were forced as well."

I debated on how to answer her statement. "I'm the next in line to lead the Allegany pack, so it's my duty to be part of the MDA."

She chuckled and glanced sideways at me. "An alpha? I would have never guessed."

I couldn't tell whether she was being coy or not.

"Why aren't you with your pack?" She nodded toward the opposite door, as if she knew where we were staying.

"Hungry. Remember?" I didn't want to come right out and say I was waiting for her to show up. That would put me in a weird category, and I didn't want her to think I was creepy.

"Mhm." She studied me out of the corner of her eye. "Have you read the handbook yet?"

"No, but I probably could recite the rules of this place to you in my sleep." I offered her a smile while my wolf pushed the boundaries of my control. I leaned forward, putting my elbows on my knees as I picked at a hangnail on my thumb as a diversion.

"Are you one of those who follows the rules religiously?" Hope bled into the lilt of her question, and I turned to meet her gaze.

There was the sign I was waiting for. She licked her lips and the light danced in her dilated eyes, making me smile. But before I could answer her, Johnson slid into the hallway.

"The cafeteria isn't open yet?" Johnson waved at the door and then he looked at his watch before he focused his attention on Sarah. "Well, hello," he said in his silky seduction voice that almost drew a growl from me. He stuck his hand out. "I'm Johnson."

"What, did your mother not like you or something?" Sarah shook his hand.

I pressed my lips together against the smirk that crept onto them. I gave Sarah a sideways glance, and her face had the same half-suppressed smile that I was trying to keep off my face.

Johnson turned red at the comment and shoved his hands in his pockets. "Johnson is my last name."

Sarah's eyebrows shot up and her mouth popped open for a split second. If I hadn't been looking at her, I never would have caught that flash of surprise. "Oh. I'm sorry." Her cheeks turned a rose color that complemented her hair.

The sound of locks releasing had us all turning toward the dining room door. When it swung open, I shot to my feet. Sarah followed and we descended on the newly laid-out buffet, heaping barbequed ribs, potatoes, and corn on the cob onto our plates and finding a seat in the back corner together.

With my back to the wall, I had a view of the entire cafeteria, from the buffet tables to the massive fireplace that had pristine birch logs stacked inside for show. The arched ceiling was broken by stained-glass windows that would paint the room with color at noon when the sun was high. Beyond the buffet setup was a raised platform with a long table waiting for the school staff to enter. I didn't give that area any more than a cursory look.

The rest of the school rushed in moments later, and the quiet solitude we had went straight to hell. I didn't get a chance to talk at any length with Sarah for the rest of the evening, even with her sitting across from me at the table. Not when the rest of the pack had joined us and monopolized the conversation. Every time my leg brushed against hers under the table, a jolt of electricity traveled from the spot we connected, shooting straight to my heart.

All I knew was when she licked the barbeque sauce off her fingers, I had to blink a few times to get myself under control. I wished it was something else she was licking like that. Johnson actually elbowed me to get me to stop staring at her.

"I should go try to get some sleep," Sarah said when her tray was empty and her eyes at half-mast of a food comma. "I want to be awake and aware when I meet my partner tomorrow."

I went to stand and offer to walk her to her room, but Johnson grabbed my knee under the table and gave me a quick shake of his head. He nodded toward the head table. A table I hadn't paid any attention to all night. My father sat near the headmaster, with his arms crossed and a scowl on his face.

Fuck.

I couldn't leave the dining room with her. Not with his complete aggravation radiating over the entire room. I turned back to Sarah, but she had already stepped away.

Double fuck.

I took a breath and gave Johnson a nod of thanks. If I had wandered off with Sarah, she would likely get booted from the school tomorrow. Although, on second thought, that might not be a bad thing. Especially if she was here under duress. If she was let go at this stage of training, there wouldn't be a single thing keeping me from claiming her.

I smacked Johnson's hand away and crossed to the exit. But by the time I pushed the door that she had first come through open, the hallway was empty, and I couldn't rightfully wander around the women's dorm looking for her.

"Shit." I had lost her.

3

THE NEXT MORNING STARTED out gray and overcast, with rain in the forecast. Not the best mood-inspiring day to meet partners, but I was just as anxious to learn who would have my back in battle.

I grabbed a quick breakfast and headed to the assembly hall and the corkboard outside the door with the list of names. I stared at the sheets on the wall announcing who our assigned partners were. My finger ran down the list and when I came to my name, my brain stalled.

I stepped back as the rest of the students slid by to read the list.

"What the actual fuck?" Words finally slipped out of my mouth, but my feet wouldn't budge. I stared at the damnation written on the board as a fiery anger filled every cell.

My father did this.

"Seriously?" Her voice rang from the spot next to me. "You're my partner?" She looked up at me. "A fucking alpha wolf?"

I glanced at her, and my gut tightened. My wolf nearly burst forth, but I kept him under wraps. Because now, if I gave in to this blinding need, it meant she would be put under the guillotine. Literally.

"Apparently." I tried to keep the hostility out of my words.

"Someone must really hate me," she muttered under her breath.

I cocked my eyebrow at her. "What's that supposed to mean?"

She squared herself in front of me, crossed her arms, and glared. "I'm not subservient to anyone."

I laughed, because she was such a perfect fit for me. I didn't want a meek bitch underfoot, and it just burned even more that my father had fucked up any chance I had with this girl.

Her eyes narrowed. "I'm serious."

"I'm not laughing at you. I promise." I glanced at the list, wondering who had been misplaced with my father's last-minute change. But there were no other female and male pairings on the list. Which meant a few candidates had been escorted off the property in the dark of night. My gaze sliced back to hers. "And I'd never try to impart my alpha influence on you."

She blinked up at me as if I had just answered whatever prayer she had engaged in the night before.

"I'm not here to control my partner. I'm here to spill a lot of vampire blood." I grinned down at her. "So, if you aren't up for that, then we *will* have a problem."

The slow, sure smile that spread over her lips, along with that insane spark in her eyes, made me curse my father even more.

"I'm totally down with that." She held out her hand. "Partner."

I didn't want to touch her, but I also didn't want to offend her, so I took her hand in a tight grip. "Here's to a lifetime of ridding vampires of their heads." My wolf nearly yanked her to my chest, but I let go of her instead. He balked at me.

Her lower lip sucked between her teeth as she glanced at the list again. "Um. Do they expect us to room together?"

When her gaze came back to mine again, all I could think about was seeing her undressed in my room. That wouldn't end well for either of us.

"My beta is my roommate." For once, I was glad for my status here. It saved me from sentencing her to death, because in that kind of intimate situation, I most certainly would not be able to control my goddamn wolf.

4

WHEN WE ENTERED THE assembly room, my father sat on stage with that smug *I know what's better for you than you do* look on his face, and a growl escaped. I maneuvered Sarah into one of the rows in the middle of the theater instead of going to the seat up front that my father no doubt reserved for me.

Sarah raised an eyebrow at me, and I shook my head. Explaining my father to her would open me up to questions I had no intentions of answering. Questions that might open a door that I so very badly wanted to keep closed.

A frown appeared on my father's face as we took a seat; his gaze slashed to the front seats and then back, as if he silently commanded me to move my ass where he wanted me to be. I pointedly sat in the seat, crossed my arms, and stared my father down. It was my declaration that he did not control me like he believed he did. I could relate to Sarah's dislike of being controlled. I hated when others fucked with my life, and my father just crossed me for the last time.

At least when my mother had been alive, she ran interference for me. She let me cultivate my friends, gain their loyalty my way. My father just wanted to beat me down and remind me I'd never be as good of a leader as he was.

"So... you and your father don't get along?" Sarah asked.

I glanced at her and sighed. "I'll never live up to his expectations."

"Sucks to be you." She leaned back in the chair and adopted the same cross-armed pose I had and gave me a curious side eye.

Damn, I wanted to take her back to my room and ravage the hell out of her. That look alone could undo my resolve, and the reality of spending the next however many years at each other's side without acting on this ache in my chest cramped my stomach. I closed my eyes and took a deep breath to get a grip on my libido and my wolf. I wanted years next to this girl. Even if it meant being just her hunting partner.

If I crossed the line, it meant *her* death.

Sudden, almost violent hatred flooded every cell like hot lava. I clenched my fists against the raw flare of rage that brushed over me like a thousand sharp claws shredding my skin. Noise filtered around us as people took their seats. When a hushed silence fell over the auditorium, I opened my eyes.

The lights over the audience dimmed and my gaze locked with my father's. Whatever smug look he entertained flashing at me fell. His expression crossed from irritation into almost alarmed, as if he read the visceral burn filling my veins, but it was gone after a few moments. The fact he needed more than a second to regain his composure pleased me. I rattled the old man.

And until this moment, my attempts at making him uncomfortable had always failed. But tonight, I nailed it. All it took was him ruining my life and my reaction to his fucking meddling to get here.

The seat next to me creaked. "There you are." Johnson slapped my shoulder as he settled in.

I grunted at him.

"Hey," he said around me.

"Hey," Sarah said with a nod of acknowledgment. "Johnson, right?"

He flashed her a smile that I wanted to pummel off his face, but she just rolled her eyes and sat back in the seat.

I sent a glare in his direction, and his smile faded.

Sarah leaned forward and hooked a thumb at me. "Are you his roommate?"

Johnson nodded, and she smirked at him.

"Good luck with Mr. Moody here." She glanced at me and leaned back in her chair.

I cocked my eyebrow at her.

"What?" she asked me. "You've been all kinds of moody since we met. It's like you're on your period or something."

Johnson snorted a laugh.

My lips crept into a smile. "I'm usually not this bad," I grumbled. But she was right. I hadn't exactly been my laid-back self around her. Not with every single cell in my body screaming at me to claim her, and knowing doing that would mean her death.

I wasn't sure I'd ever be myself again.

5

I PACED ACROSS THE floor in our room as Johnson droned on.

"Even if you claim her, she'll be executed, and you'll be exiled from the pack."

"I am fully aware of what the consequences are." I knew, but I kept searching for a way around them. Even if I did ascend to the alpha of our pack, it wouldn't mean a thing. If I crossed the line, she'd be sentenced to death. The MDA did not spare witches, and in their eyes, a rogue wolf was just as dangerous. So, if I broke the rules, my life as I knew it would be over.

But that didn't stop the burning desire filling me. That didn't stop my wolf from demanding I take her. "You have no idea what it feels like being near her. It drives my wolf insane." I ran my hand through my hair and threw myself down on the bed.

"Dude, you've got to control your wolf."

Johnson stating the obvious just made my blood boil even more. "My father broke MDA protocol."

"Yeah, but your mom wasn't his partner."

It's as if my father schooled him in every possible answer. Although it was true, it still burned.

"Get some sleep, Robby. Classes start early." Johnson turned off his light and was snoring within minutes.

I stared at the ceiling for what seemed like hours, playing over every option in my head, and they all led to the same place.

Losing my true mate.

"Fuck," I mumbled and rolled onto my side, hating my father even more with every passing second.

A SHRILL RING PENETRATED my head, and I reached out, slamming the snooze button. Morning had come way too fast—but then again, I tossed and turned most of the night.

Today started the living hell I would have to endure for the rest of my life. Or at least until I retired. Then, and only then, could I act on this insane need rampaging through me. It was a bitter pill to swallow.

The alarm rang again, and I swatted it, sitting up and grumbling. Johnson stepped out of the bathroom and gave me a raised eyebrow.

"I know, I'm moving." I grabbed my clothes and towel, and headed into the bathroom to clean up. My stomach rumbled, and I hurried through my morning routine. I was going to need a decent breakfast and a gallon of coffee to get through the day without nodding off.

The cafeteria was full of students, and the buffet had been sufficiently picked over by the time we got there. I surveyed the room and found the crop of red hair in the masses, wondering who her roommate was because everyone else had chosen to pair up with their partners, with the exception of me and my beta.

I piled food on my plate, grabbed the biggest coffee, and headed toward the red hair sitting at the end of one of the tables away from everyone else.

Johnson cleared his throat behind me, and I glanced at him. He nodded toward the table with the rest of my pack.

I huffed. "Go find your partner. We're supposed to be using downtime to bond with them. Or didn't you read the program booklet?" At least I had that going for me. It was expected to spend the time away from class with partners, but they had never before paired a male and female together, until this year. Besides, my wolf was pulling me toward her and right now, in this crowded room, it was the safest place to give in to his needs.

I put my tray down, and she looked up at me with those wide brown eyes that I could get lost in. Her lips morphed from the frown she wore as she stared at her food to that dazzling smile that made my brain stall.

I sat down, feeling my face crack with a smile just as bright as hers. "So, who's your roommate?" I looked around the cafeteria before I dug into my food.

"I have my own room. I guess there isn't any other female who isn't paired up." She shrugged but didn't seem too put out by not having to share her space.

"Does that bother you?" My attention returned to her, and I swear she radiated a citrus scent that made my mouth water and my mind wander.

She leaned forward. "I actually like it, but don't tell anyone because I have a feeling they would change that in a heartbeat if they knew."

I pressed my lips against a smirk. "And you're telling the alpha prick you have as a partner this because?" I raised an eyebrow at her.

She blinked and leaned back in her seat. Her mouth popped open in a little O as if she realized it wasn't prudent to trust me.

That was not my intention. I needed her to trust me, just like she needed me to trust her. If we didn't, we would fail out in the real world. I knew I'd have her back, even if it was to my detriment, but if she didn't feel that same loyalty, then I was screwed. "Don't worry, I won't say a thing," I whispered and couldn't help the grin that formed when her eyebrows lowered into a scowl.

"Asshole," she muttered and picked at her food.

"Yes. But I'm the asshole who has your back." I pointed my fork at her. "You aren't hungry?" I asked after she moved the food around her plate again.

"It's not Starbucks." She shrugged.

I belted out a laugh and almost sprayed my food all over her. "Your parents let you go to Starbucks?" My father never let me go to the fast-food places near our pack lands. He said it was poison to our bodies.

"My parents are dead."

Well, that was a conversation killer. "I'm sorry. I didn't know."

"If they were alive, I wouldn't be here."

Deep down, I cursed the fact they were dead. If she wasn't here, there would be no stopping me from claiming her as my mate.

"But the state saw fit to hand me over to get me off their hands." She continued to pick at her food, stealing glances at me, as if she were gauging my reaction.

"You like to cause trouble?"

A secret smile appeared, and she looked up at me. "If you could have anything in the world right now, what would it be?"

Such a loaded question, and I had to actually bite my tongue to keep from saying what I truly wanted. That would open a dangerous door. "I am unsure how to answer that," I finally said.

"Come on, you must want something. A designer watch, a pair of cowboy boots to go with your high and mighty attitude, a leather coat?" She took a bite of her toast, daring me to say something.

I shrugged, thinking about my motorcycle gear. "Leather sounds good." I started to lean back but froze when a deep-brown leather coat settled on my shoulders. I stared at my arms and then moved my gaze to hers.

"But I prefer a wicked knife." She held her hand out and a blade appeared in her palm. "I conjure things. Pulling them from who knows where." She put her knife down by her plate and smiled.

"So, the answer to my question is yes. You like to stir the pot." I smiled. "What would you have done if I said I wanted a Maserati?"

She shrugged. "I would have told you to look outside." Her smile faded. "The thing is, I'm not sure if I'm creating this stuff out of thin air or if it exists and I'm just pulling it to me."

"So... stealing?" I cringed as I asked, but it certainly was an intriguing ability.

"I'd like to think I'm creating it and not stealing it, but I have no clue." She sent the knife back to wherever it came from but she left the leather on me.

I bit my lip and cocked an eyebrow. "What about a horse?"

She shook her head. "I'm limited to *things*. I can't conjure anything living. Which sucks, because I'd love to have a big-ass dog to play with."

The way she said that turned me on. "Well, you've got yourself a big-ass wolf to hunt vampires with. So, in a way, you got your wish."

Her cheeks reddened, and she preoccupied herself with downing her coffee. Then she grimaced, setting the cup aside. A blink later, a Starbucks coffee sat in her hand. "I can't drink that stuff." She nodded toward her nearly full cup.

God, why the hell did my father curse me like this? I shifted in my seat and focused on my food, finishing my meal before wiping my lips with a napkin like my mother taught me. I looked up to her studying me over the rim of her coffee cup and wished like hell I could read her mind.

"We should get to class." I piled up the garbage on my tray. I reached for hers just as she did. "I got it." I took her tray, too. It gave me a minute to compose myself, and I took a deep breath as I threw away the papers and leftover food from her plate before stacking the trays on the conveyor belt that would take them to the kitchen for cleaning.

I harnessed my wolf and turned back toward Sarah. She stood waiting for me, bathed in a streak of sunlight; her hair looked as if it were on fire and that half smile on her lips nearly cut my legs out from underneath me. As I approached her, Johnson walked in our direction, along with someone I didn't recognize. Behind him, the pack followed with their partners.

Sarah stepped in stride with me as we led the group out of the cafeteria. She glanced over her shoulder and then up at me with a raised eyebrow as my pack followed.

"It's a pack thing," I said quietly as if that explained the weirdness of them all converging on me like I was their king or something equally as special. I wanted to lead, but didn't want to be treated like royalty. I'd have to have a word with them later, because this was an embarrassing display of follow the leader.

Classes went by in a blur, and I was glad to have something else to occupy my mind, even if I was hyper-aware of Sarah next to me the entire time. Learning the history of creatures like Pegasus and the phoenix, which no longer existed, was intriguing. Hell, it could be werewolves or witches or fae on that list someday.

But my life's mission was to put vampires on the extinct list.

6

DAY IN AND DAY out, I fought with my wolf as I sat next to Sarah in class or sparred with her in our self-defense classes. During the physical sessions when we were paired up, I never let loose. I never attacked her with my full strength.

"You're holding back," she snarled at me. "How the hell am I supposed to defend myself out there if you won't come at me with all you have?" She wiped the sweat off her brow with the back of her hand and snapped it onto the ground.

My lips tilted into a smile. "If I went full out, I'd rip your head clean off."

"Bullshit!" She swung at me, and I caught her fist in mine, displaying exactly what type of speed I was capable of.

This time, instead of letting her go, I pulled her against me and stared down at her. "Trust me, sweetheart. You do not want me letting loose on you or anyone else here." The growl in my voice was more feral than even I expected.

Her eyes widened as she glanced up at me, and her pupils dilated like being this close to me did the same thing to her. And it wasn't fear I saw in those irises; it was the same heat burning through my veins.

Damn it.

My wolf rose to the surface, and my teeth transformed. I let go of her and stepped back, getting a grip on my wolf before he took over completely.

Johnson barreled into me from the side, taking me to the ground with a roar. It was sudden enough to make me lose my tenuous control. I shifted and turned on him, baring my teeth in a feral growl.

My wolf was ready for a serious beating, and I was going to be the one who drew first blood.

Johnson shifted a moment later, growling with the same ferocity.

Sarah stepped between us, putting her palms on either side of her, one facing me and the other facing Johnson. My growl stalled at her audacity.

You never step between two wolves getting ready to tango. Ever.

"Cut the crap!" She glared at us and then focused on Johnson. "You want a fight?" She slammed her hands on her chest. "Come at me. Let's see what you've got." A pair of wooden swords appeared in her hands, and she stood at the ready like some ninja queen. When Johnson didn't move, she said, "He won't go at me with everything he has. Maybe you're just as much of a wuss."

I bared my teeth at him, wanting to keep her from harm, but Johnson didn't even look my way. He stalked toward her and then launched, but Sarah twirled away, parrying, and slammed the side of her sword into Johnson's shoulder, knocking his trajectory off so he sailed right past her.

Fuck. That just turned on my wolf to a degree I couldn't harness and ignited my need to protect her.

The next time Johnson leapt at her, I launched into his side, knocking him away, and turned on her. If she wanted to play this game, who was I to argue?

"Oh. Now you want to play?" she teased as the rest of the class stopped their own sparring to watch this unfold. Her eyes sparkled and her grin heated me to the core.

I stalked around her, letting a low growl form in my throat. Johnson stalked opposite me, but I wasn't sure whether he was there to test my partner, or keep me in line. Either way the two-on-one seemed to make Sarah thrive. The skin of her chest flushed as if this excited her as much as it revved me up. She held the swords out from her sides, keeping them between us, and she matched our slow maneuvers around her.

Johnson wasn't as patient as I was for an opening, and he launched. Sarah parried, doing the same move as before, but he was ready and he yanked the sword from her grip, opening her up to my attack. I launched, hitting her square in the chest, and knocked her onto her back. I shifted my paws, pinning her upper arms.

Then the tip of her sword pressed between my ribs at my side.

"It might not be a kill shot, but it will scramble your insides, so I suggest you get the fuck off me before I shish-kebab you." She stared up at me with such ferociousness that I had to clamp my mouth closed, or else I was going to lick that look right off her face.

Fuck. I wanted this girl.

I sidestepped and then snatched the sword from her, tossing it away. When I looked back, I was staring down real steel in one hand as her other pointed a sword at Johnson. I traded a glance with my beta and then stepped back. He did the same as she sat up and then, with a quick and very impressive jump, she landed on her feet, still brandishing the steel swords in our direction.

Johnson shifted to human form and some of the ladies in the room gasped at his nakedness. It was part of the deal. When we shifted, it basically shredded our clothing; therefore, when we shift back, we're as naked as the day we were born. We hadn't covered werewolves yet in class, either, so I guess the witches who weren't familiar with us would just have to get used to it.

Sarah raised her eyebrow and then looked at me, expecting a full-Monty view. Well, she wasn't going to get that, not when I was so fucking turned on by her that I'd never be able to mask my desire. Instead, I trotted out of the room and shifted when I got to my locker, where I had stashed extra clothing just for this type of scenario.

I splashed cold water on my face at the sink, getting my libido in order as Johnson stepped into the room.

"What are you doing?" he asked as he retrieved a pair of shorts to cover himself up.

"Cooling myself off," I answered.

"She's going to see you shift back at some point." He waved toward the gym, correctly analyzing my retreat.

"No shit. But not when I'm so fucking hard that I can't hide it," I mumbled through the towel covering my face. I pulled the towel down and closed my eyes.

"You need to get laid," Johnson said.

I snorted a laugh and nodded. "But that's not happening here."

"Some of the guys were already talking about a road trip to the city tomorrow." He glanced at me. "Are you in?"

"Fuck yeah." I needed to get out of this place and as far away from the stress pulling my insides apart as possible.

We headed back into the gym again, and only the instructor, Mr. Martin, and our partners were in attendance. Mr. Martin's face was pinched in irritation and his blond spiked hair was cockeyed, as if he had been running his hand through it in aggravation. He shifted his spectacles at us as we approached; crossing his arms, he scowled.

Sarah stared at the floor with her cheeks the color of crimson wine.

Mr. Martin pointed at the two of us, his finger slashing back and forth like a pendulum. "That was not sanctioned. You could have gotten hurt!"

"Chill, Grandpa," I said. "We wouldn't have harmed her."

His face reddened until I thought steam would pop the top off. "You're a werewolf, and she's just a girl."

I crossed into his personal space and glared down at him. "I'm an alpha. I know the strengths and weaknesses of my pack, *and* my partner. We would not have harmed her."

"She has a bump on the back of her head where she hit the ground," he challenged, puffing out his chest like a cockatoo.

I slashed my gaze to Sarah, and she rolled her eyes like it was no big deal. "Bumps and bruises are part of sparring." I looked back at our instructor. "Aren't they?"

"She could have sliced you with those swords and spilled blood." Mr. Martin still seethed, as if my question annoyed him even more than our actions.

"I'm her partner. She has my back, just like I have hers. And if she inadvertently sliced us, well, we weren't quick enough, and that's our problem, not yours."

"You three are on probation until I see fit to release you."

I shrugged, and Johnson pulled me back a step.

"Does that mean we can't leave campus this weekend?" he asked.

"Correct. You can only go to classes, the library, the gym, and the cafeteria. The rest of the time, you are to stay in your rooms. No joining in on the games in the quad, no running on the paths, nothing. And certainly no leaving campus."

"Fuck," he muttered under his breath and glared at me.

Sarah's face fell. "I had plans."

"Your plans are canceled until I say so," Mr. Martin snarled. "Now go clean up for dinner."

Sarah took a deep breath and marched toward the door. I caught up with her and grabbed her arm. She spun around on me and smacked my bare chest hard enough to sting.

"You should have given me your all during class and not made a fucking spectacle of it." She yanked her arm from my grip and stormed into the girls' showers, leaving me staring after her.

Now I needed to know just what her plans were, and if there was a guy involved. The insidious burn of jealousy caught me off guard. I spun on my heel and headed back to my room with my wolf in an uproar.

"What the fuck were you thinking?" Johnson growled when I stepped into the room.

"You're the one who tackled me out of nowhere." I slammed the door behind me.

"You were stepping over the line," he mumbled.

"I was in control."

"Bull-fucking-shit!" He pointed at me. "Your wolf was already coming out. You were not in control."

My teeth had made an appearance when I slammed her into me. "I was aggravated." But my tone didn't convince even me of that excuse. I clawed my fingers through my hair. "I had control," I finally said, but the skeptical scowl on Johnson's face echoed what I knew in my heart.

This entire situation was out of control. I grabbed clean clothes and headed into the shower without another word. I dialed the knob as cold as it would go, shaking under the icy water as my teeth chattered and the chill bit me bone-deep. I scrubbed my skin and lathered and rinsed my hair, forcing myself to deal with the chilling water.

But the frigid shower didn't even come close to dousing the fire in the center of my soul.

7

THE MINUTE I STEPPED into the cafeteria, the whispering stopped. Johnson followed after me. It wasn't until I sat down with the pack that I realized Sarah wasn't here. I scanned the room just to be sure and then sighed, digging into my meal with all the gusto of an inmate on death row.

Sarah still hadn't come when they started to close the food stations. I got up and packed a plate to go. When I returned to the table with a cellophane-wrapped dinner plate, Johnson raised an eyebrow.

I didn't dignify his silent question with an answer. "I'll be back upstairs in a few," I said to him. "And I don't need a shadow. Understand." My gaze bore into him, but I refrained from using my alpha influence. I hated it when my father did that, and I wasn't going to do it to my beta unless I had to.

"Fine. But it's her funeral if you fuck up."

"I know." I turned and headed out of the cafeteria. Instead of heading left to my section, I turned right and wandered through the girls' ward, using my nose to try to find Sarah's room.

A group of girls armed with backpacks sauntered down the hall toward me.

"Do you know which room is Sarah Stone's?" I asked because it was easier than following my nose, especially considering the hallway was filled with everyone's scent. Besides, I wasn't in wolf form, so I couldn't quite pinpoint hers among the rest.

The lead girl pointed behind her. "Last door on your right."

"Thanks." I gave her a nod.

"You could get in trouble for being in this wing," she said as she passed by.

"It's a good thing no one is going to rat me out, right?" This time, I did use my alpha influence, and the girls seemed to fold in on themselves and almost cower at the power I radiated.

"Right," the lead one said in a wince.

The door at the end of the hall opened. "What the hell are you doing?" Sarah asked, as if she could feel my alpha influence all the way down the hall. Her voice was slurred but the glare she gave me was sharp.

The rest of the girls hurried off without so much as a look in our direction. I continued down the hall with the plate in front of me, undeterred by my partner's piercing look. But the closer I got, the more she reeked of alcohol. No wonder I couldn't pick up her scent—it was doused in vodka.

"I don't need food." She started to close her door.

I stopped the wood with my hand. "I beg to differ." I pushed her inside and closed the door behind me, painfully aware of how close she was to me. But below that feisty anger was a deeper pain that I couldn't walk away from now that I saw it. "Where did you get alcohol?" I scanned the room for any evidence of it.

She put her hand out and a half-empty bottle appeared. "I'm a witch. Or did you forget that?"

I crossed and put the plate down on her desk. When I turned, she had the bottle tipped to her lips and was guzzling it like it was water. The shock of seeing her nearly drowning herself in liquor made me reach out and snatch the bottle from her.

"Easy there."

"What the fuck do you know?" She pushed at my chest. "Give me that."

I raised it over my head. "No. Not until you tell me what the hell is wrong enough for you to get hammered in a place where if they caught you, you'd be in a shit ton of trouble."

"It's none of your business," she snarled, still trying to get the bottle.

"What, did I ruin a weekend with your boyfriend?"

"No, you asshole. You ruined my chance to visit my parents' grave."

Her words hit me hard, and I slowly lowered the bottle. Handing it to her, I took a seat on the empty bed. "I'm sorry. I didn't know."

She shook her head and stared at the bottle. "They died in a car crash last year. Today's the anniversary of their death."

Quiet layered over the room.

"Think you can conjure me a glass?"

A moment later, a cup appeared in my hand, and I held it out nodding toward the bottle.

"You could get in trouble," she said.

"Fuck it. This is a valid reason for a drink."

She filled my cup halfway, and I raised my glass. "To your parents. May they be filled with heaven's joy and peace for all eternity." I touched my glass to her bottle in a toast and downed the contents of the cup. The smooth burn of vodka flowed down my throat, hitting my stomach, and sent a rash of heat all the way to my toes and fingertips.

She stared at me as a tear escaped, sliding down her cheek unchecked. "Losing them nearly killed me," she said, searching my eyes.

I nodded. I knew the impact of losing a parent. Especially one you were close to. But this wasn't about me or how I felt when a vampire ripped my mother from this earth. I would be able to purge that anger with every vampire I killed in this job.

"What happened?" I stared into my cup, ignoring my wolf's demands to hold her. If I moved any closer, I'd be in a hell of a lot more trouble than just drinking with my partner.

"A car crash on their date night." She let out a soft laugh. "They still did date nights after almost twenty years of marriage. Can you believe that?" She sniffled and stared into the bottle.

"Sounds like they were still in love." My heart squeezed at the thought. I couldn't imagine that at all. Although my parents cared about each other as fated mates do, they never truly showed it. There were no date nights in my home. Just the alpha bastard demanding all of us be subservient, including my mother. The only times she stood up to him was when she didn't agree with how he was treating me or my siblings.

"Do you have any other family out there?" I asked, knowing it was a long shot.

She shook her head. "Nope. No siblings. No long-lost aunts or uncles. No living grandparents. Nothing. And I've been in state facilities for the last year. Until I turned sixteen and the state decided I was best suited for the Monster Defense Academy." She glared up at me. "So now I have to hunt monsters until I die instead of being a doctor or lawyer and finding someone to settle down and have date nights with."

My lips tilted into a partial smile. "Yeah. Like being a doctor or lawyer is the same as a monster hunter. You can't literally kick ass in those vocations."

She pouted in a way that made my hands clench. I wanted to suck on her lower lip and make her forget all her pain. But that would only make things worse. I took a deep breath.

"Maybe," she finally allowed and glanced at the plate of food. "Thank you." She waved at the dinner I brought her. "You didn't need to do that."

When her brown eyes met mine, I nearly slid off the bed onto my knees and begged her to be mine. But I formed a smile and remained seated across the room. "It wasn't a problem." I shrugged. "It's part of being partners." That was the best crap I could come up with. "You should go easy on the rest of that bottle. You don't need alcohol poisoning on top of everything else."

Her gaze narrowed, and she took a swig. "I can handle it."

I let out a laugh. "I'm not saying you can't, but straight vodka for a woman your size is bound to play hell with your system if you drink too much. And I'd kind of like to see you in action out there. I bet you're one of the fiercest women here." Actually, I knew she was just by watching her sparring matches over the last month and a half.

"I am the fiercest one here." She flipped her hair over her shoulder and straightened her back.

I leaned forward. "Be fierce. Ditch the rest of that bottle," I dared her.

She looked at the vodka and then waved the bottle away. Her chin jutted out at me as if she had done something incredibly fierce.

I couldn't help it; I snorted a laugh and she started to chuckle as well until she fell backward on her bed laughing so hard, I couldn't tell whether she was hysterical with the funnies or hysterical from missing her parents.

She held her stomach, silently shaking with her face buried in her bedding. I stood and took a step closer as concern replaced my jovial mood. She stiffened and glanced up at me, still smiling as she wiped tears from her cheeks.

"I haven't laughed like that since before my parents died." Her voice shook with her continued giggles. "Thank you. For making me laugh. For the food... everything. But if you get any closer, I'm not responsible enough right now *not* to do anything we will both regret in the morning."

I froze in the spot as my mind toggled between "make a damn move" and "get the hell out of this room now." When she hiccupped between chuckles, that seemed to get my legs moving.

"I'll catch you tomorrow," I said over my shoulder and walked out of the room, heading across to my dorm as the need to ravage her screamed in my veins like an incessant echo that would never die.

8

"**I** HATE MY FATHER." The words came out with such venom that Johnson's eyes widened from across the room. I slammed the door behind me and crossed, throwing myself face-first on the bed.

"Hate's a strong word, dude."

"You have no fucking clue how much I want to beat him to a bloody pulp right now." I turned my head away before I tore into him for doing my father's bidding.

"If I could denounce him without denouncing the pack, I would," I muttered. At this point, my best bet was becoming the alpha of the pack. Then I wouldn't have to listen to anything the old man said.

"He's still on the board of the Monster Defense Agency," Johnson said.

I turned and glared at him. "He could change the rules if he wanted, but he'll never do that. He'd rather see my true mate hanging from the gallows than in a relationship with me."

"You don't know that."

"Who the fuck do you think arranged for Sarah to be my partner?" I moved up to my elbows, waiting for him to answer. "Who do you think chose to fuck up my entire life?" I raised my eyebrows. "Because it certainly wasn't me."

"I get it. But it is what it is, and you need to move on." He closed the textbook he had been reading when I stormed into the room.

Johnson didn't have a clue. He hadn't met his true mate yet and didn't begin to comprehend the demands my wolf was making. I was surprised my father didn't have any sympathy for me, but then again, Sarah wasn't a wolf. I rolled onto my back. *If she had been a werewolf, would he have moved heaven and earth to interfere?*

I already knew the answer to that question. He wouldn't have interfered.

My father's racism stemmed from the fact Sarah was a witch and not a wolf.

BREAKFAST THE NEXT MORNING was nearly empty. A whole dozen of us remained at the school—the bad kids or the rejects with nowhere else to go. I piled the food on my plate and started for the table Johnson had chosen.

Sarah walked in with dark sunglasses, her hair braided, and a black leather outfit that nearly had me stumbling. She looked like a killer version of Laura Croft. But her red braid made her look even more badass. I caught myself before my mouth dropped open, and I just raised an eyebrow.

"If you're trying to look the part of troublemaker, you nailed it," I muttered as she approached.

She slid her glasses down her nose as she got closer, showing me her bloodshot eyes. "I'm compensating," she whispered. "And you don't have to yell."

I smirked. "Hangover?"

"From hell." She continued on to the buffet, poured an extra-large cup of coffee, and grabbed a single piece of toast along with a canned ginger ale before she headed to our table.

It wasn't much, but I guess if I had drunk two-thirds of a bottle of vodka on my own, I'd be hurting too. I took a seat next to Johnson and a few minutes later, Sarah sat down opposite me.

Johnson's eyes were just about bugging out of his head at her. Just like the rest of the crew stuck at the school this weekend. Hell, even the lone she-wolf looked at her with a spark of interest.

Ignoring my wolf's rantings was getting harder to do, especially with the citrusy scent drifting off her like a natural elixir. Man, I wanted to lick her just to see whether she tasted as sweet as she smelled. I focused on my food instead.

"Young lady, what the hell are you wearing?" Mr. Martin snarled from behind her.

I looked up at her and then at the teacher seething behind her.

Sarah straightened her back and slowly turned in her chair. "I'm wearing clothing fit for kicking his ass." She pointed at me. "Which I fully intend to do after breakfast."

I choked on the sip of coffee, spitting all over the table. "Excuse me?" I said through my coughs.

"I don't..." the teacher started.

"He owes me." She glared at him. "I had plans that this wolf fucked up. So, with or without your permission, sir, I am going to beat his ass to a pulp. And I'm going to do it in my kick-ass outfit."

She oozed attitude that even I wouldn't fuck with.

Mr. Martin pressed his lips together, and his face reddened as she stared him down through her dark glasses.

Now she was going to get reamed. I waited for the explosive reprimand.

He clenched his teeth and wagged his finger at her. "No sharp weapons."

What the fuck did he just say? My brain didn't think I heard him right.

"No, sir. I won't use sharp weapons." She nodded and turned back to me with the type of grin that made me want another frigid shower.

His glare shot to me. "And no wolf. Save that for the field, understand?"

I was so fucked. "Yes, sir," I hissed while my lungs still burned with the coffee that had slid the wrong way.

He pointed at Johnson. "And no sabotaging their sparring."

Johnson shook his head and held up his hand. "I swear."

Mr. Martin dropped his gaze back on Sarah. "A bit of advice. You should keep your fighting gear for the gym to avoid potential problems."

I cocked my head. "What potential problems? Relationships are off-limits here."

His gaze slashed to mine. "Exactly. And everyone needs to remember that." He scanned the whole dozen of us who remained in the cafeteria with a pointed scowl.

"And what happens if we cross the line?" the female wolf asked, drawing everyone's attention.

Mr. Martin turned to her. "The consequences are swift and severe. We own every one of your asses until you either retire or you die in the field. Get used to living, or dying, by the rules."

She scoffed at him, and Mr. Martin cut his glare at her. That little wolf started clawing at her throat as if she couldn't breathe.

He crossed to stand in front of her. His eyes sparkled with malice. "Dear Miss Carlyle, if you don't learn to respect the rules here, your partner will pay the price. Hunting solo is a deadly endeavor for a witch."

"Leave her be." I pushed my alpha voice over the dining room. It had the desired effect and Miss Carlyle took a hefty breath as tears of fear and disdain cascaded down her face.

Mr. Martin wouldn't look at me, he glared at the floor, though and I felt the brush of his angry magic as he made a beeline out of the room. The only one in the vicinity who wasn't cowering in some fashion was Sarah.

I cocked my head at her, and she pointed a finger at me.

"I'm subservient to no one. Remember that, alpha boy. I'll see you in the gym in ten minutes." She stood and marched out of the room.

"Alpha boy?" Johnson whispered from the spot next to me.

"She's still pissed because I ruined her weekend plans." I stood and scooped up my nearly empty tray. I set it on the rotating cleaning rack and headed to my room to change. A little fiery witch needed to meet the training mat today, and I prayed my wolf would stay in line.

9

I STEPPED INTO THE gym in my T-shirt and shorts. She was already doing forms on the mat like a trained ninja. Her leathers didn't seem to prohibit her movement, either. The bo she held whistled through the air with each twirl. I paused and then peeled off my sneakers and socks, lining them up near the door, getting myself mentally ready for close contact.

We weren't the only ones in the gym, either. All the students from the cafeteria were sitting quietly on the edges as if we were the main entertainment for the day.

I stepped into the sparring ring and bowed to Sarah.

She stopped her forms, bowed, and then smiled. "Are you going to give me your all today?"

I stalked forward. "I don't plan on holding back, so get ready for some broken bones, missy."

She slowly twirled the staff in her hands as she countered each of my steps, moving us into a tighter circle. "Me? I think you're going to be the one who breaks. But whether it's your bones or your ego, we'll find out."

Oh, she was cocky. Even with flawless forms, she'd never be able to nail me with that bo. I clenched my fists, tapping into my endless sexual frustration, turning it into fuel. I went after her, and she countered every single one of my moves—parrying, spinning, jumping, and swinging that bo like an ISKA World Champion.

When she went on the offensive, even my speed wasn't enough. She landed her first hit with a swing of the bo into the back of my knee, and I went down with the force of it. I caught myself before my face hit the mat and rolled, coming up on my feet—only to be smacked again, but this time on the back of the other thigh. Pain flared like a nest of bees had stung me where she hit. I spun and ducked before the next swing nearly connected with the side of my head.

"You've been holding out on me," I said through clenched teeth. She had never landed a hit in training class. But then again, I never went after her with the full force of my skills.

"I didn't think your pack would take kindly to me beating the shit out of their alpha." She smiled in such a way that revved my wolf. She swung again, this time going for my shins, and I jumped, but she already calculated my move and brought the stick up, nailing my shins anyway.

I launched forward and tucked, rolling onto my back with legs that I could tell would sport some ugly bruises tomorrow. "You wouldn't get a lick in against my wolf." I stared up at her as she stood just out of range, twirling the bo from hand to hand, leaving no chance for me to jump to my feet and get a hit in.

"Prove it."

"Did you just dare me?" I rolled over onto all fours and glared at her.

She grinned. "I dare you."

That was the last straw. My wolf took over even though Mr. Martin yelled from the sideline. But this time, Johnson had my back. He held Mr. Martin on the sidelines.

I growled at Sarah, watching the bo and not her sparkling eyes. If I looked at her eyes, I would knock her to the floor and mark her as mine. My wolf didn't quite get that would be her end. He would fight to the death defending her, but it wouldn't be enough. Not with the archaic rules of this organization.

My muscles tensed as she twirled her body toward me, her bo spinning at almost an invisible speed. She swung and I reacted, dodging to the side, but it wasn't fast enough. The end of her bo connected with my ribs, knocking a yelp out of me. My wolf took over and went after her with all the fury locked inside me.

She switched to defensive moves, and her eyes widened. The first flare of fear reached the surface, and it smelled sweet. Especially when I caught the bo between my teeth and yanked it from her hands. My wolf launched and my paws connected with her shoulders, knocking her backward with the force.

Time slowed, and I flew with her.

Shit. My partner was going to hit the wood floor. Not the mat. And it would be hard enough to split her skull wide open. I shifted, putting my hand under her head just in time to protect her from the bulk of impact. Her head slammed my hand into the wood and the crack of bone filled the auditorium. I clenched my jaw against the flare of pain that traveled from my hand up my arm as my full weight landed on top of her.

I let out a hiss as her wide eyes met mine. "Fuck," I growled and pulled my hand out from under her head, and rolled off her, curling up on my side as I cradled my broken hand.

Better my hand than her head. That kind of impact could have killed her.

"Robby?" Her warm hand landed on my shoulder, and I looked up at her as a pleasant burn radiated from the point her skin made contact with mine.

Concern painted her face and her gaze seemed to flit over my naked form, as if she didn't understand where my clothes had gone. I had run into the men's locker room as a wolf before, so she hadn't seen me shift back.

"This is what happens when a wolf shifts back to human," I said, still cradling my throbbing hand against my chest. *How many bones had I broken?*

Her lips twitched and that smirk made an appearance as if she enjoyed the view just a little too much. "Is your hand okay?" she asked after a moment.

"At least one of the bones is broken. Your head is pretty damn hard," I said. I couldn't let her think I had softened in any way, regardless of the electrical current flowing from her fingers right to my soul.

"So I've been told." She actually looked remorseful. "You didn't have to do that."

I gave her a genuine smile despite the sharp pains shooting up my arm. She might not be here if I hadn't. "It's what partners do. I'll always have your back. Even when I'm the one who put you in harm's way."

Johnson threw one of the gym tarps over me, interrupting. I didn't know whether to be pissed off or grateful.

"I told you not to shift!" Mr. Martin yelled, wagging his finger at me again as he approached.

"I dared him to," Sarah said, with her hand still on my shoulder.

She squeezed a fraction tighter, as if her nerves were finally getting to her. I don't think she was aware she was doing it either, but the connection of skin against skin stirred my wolf, and I was thankful for the tarp. I adjusted it and sat up, dislodging her touch and making that electric hum assaulting my body stop.

Her declaration silenced the teacher for a moment, and he looked truly shocked. "Do you have a death wish?" He ran a hand through his hair. "You never dare a wolf to come forth. That's just asking for trouble."

She shrugged. "He wasn't giving me his all."

I snorted a laugh. "Actually, I was. You're the one who's been holding back this whole time." I waved my good hand toward the bo. "You're fucking fast with that thing. And I mean like ninja fast."

Her gaze snapped to mine, and her eyebrows rose.

"Where did you learn that?" Mr. Martin's momentary annoyance transitioned to interest just a little too fast for my tastes. It was as if he were looking at his student in a totally new light.

"I've been taking jujitsu since I was old enough to walk. But I'm a little rusty. I haven't been in the dojo for a while." She glanced at me and narrowed her eyes.

I huffed. If this was her in rusty form, then anyone she came across out in the field was as doomed as my heart was. There were some benefits to having a fucking ninja warrior as a partner. Although, I still would much rather have her as my mate.

"Why did you stop?" Mr. Martin asked.

"State care doesn't support it." She stood and offered me her hand. "So, I never got my third-degree black belt."

"I'm good." I waved her off. If I stood with her help, I wouldn't have a hand to keep the blanket in place, which had been more necessary as each moment passed.

"At sixteen?" Mr. Martin scoffed at her.

"I'm almost seventeen. And yes. That's fourteen years of study."

His eyes narrowed. "They usually don't let those under eighteen obtain black belt, never mind degrees in belts."

She crossed her arms and glared at him. "It was my father's dojo."

"And where is your father today?" he asked.

"Dead and buried. Which is why I've been sentenced to this place for the rest of my life." Her venom had all of us leaning away from her, as if her toxic attitude were somehow contagious.

The way Mr. Martin paled made me nearly laugh out loud. He thought she had something to do with her father's death. I could see it in the fear that bloomed in his eyes and the stench he was emitting.

I cleared my throat. "I think we need to get an x-ray on my hand." I held it up for him to see. The back of my hand was noticeably red, and it had swelled enough to confirm what I already knew. At least one of the metacarpal bones had cracked.

"Take him to the infirmary," Mr. Martin spat at Johnson and then turned back to Sarah. "And you and I will need to update your records, so I know your skill level." He pointed toward his office.

Johnson helped me to my feet and held the blanket closed behind me as we headed into the locker room. I caught Sarah's glance just as she and Mr. Martin disappeared into his office.

"She's deadly," Johnson whispered as we stepped up to my locker. He opened it and handed me another set of spare clothing.

The awe in his voice caught me, and I grabbed him with my good hand, slamming him against the metal. "Don't even think it. Understand?" The thought of anyone here at the academy touching her drove me crazy. If they did, it put her in danger, and my protection instinct where she was concerned was obviously stronger than my desire.

He nodded and swallowed hard. "Sure, Robby. I won't even entertain the idea." He put his hands up in surrender, and I let him go.

I dressed and headed to the infirmary and a cast that had my name on it. But my unease at the way both Johnson and Mr. Martin had been gawking at Sarah had my stomach in knots.

Johnson wouldn't do anything. He was bound by my alpha orders, and I gave him a direct order not to even think about getting into Sarah's pants.

But Mr. Martin was a different beast. I didn't know whether he had to follow the same rules we were bound by. *And if he did, would he care about the ramifications?*

The thought chilled me, and I let out a growl, startling the medical tech who was now wrapping my hand in plaster.

10

THE BEATDOWN SARAH GAVE me became somewhat of a legend at the academy once the students came back from their weekend furlough. Sarah proved to be one of the best fighters in the class, beating wolves and witches as if they were children play fighting with the adults. And I had to sit on the sidelines watching, like a fucking invalid.

However, seeing her fight with the grace of a dancer and the brutality of a natural killer inspired a sense of awe and pride in me. It was almost as acute as the want in my bones. I was damn glad she was my partner.

"So, when do you get that off?" Sarah asked in that breathless way she had when she had exerted herself. She sat on the bench next to me and pointed at my cast.

Her tone crawled under my skin, scratching at the binds holding my wolf back. Her hair dripped from perspiration and strands stuck to her face. I had to clench my fist so I didn't follow through on the urge to tuck those stray hairs behind her ear. Even as sweaty as she was, she still had that sweet citrusy scent underneath, teasing me to the breaking point.

"Next week." I glanced at the dirty plaster encasing my forearm and hand and, as if on cue, my wrist started to itch. And that itch just kept growing. My finger couldn't reach it either, so I pulled a pen out of my notebook and shoved it into the cast. Even that didn't quite reach it, but that didn't stop me from trying.

Sarah cleared her throat and gave me that look that stopped me cold. It was her *don't do that* expression that I couldn't ignore.

I sighed and slipped the pen back where I pulled it from.

"Then what? Physical therapy?"

"That's what they tell me." I wasn't all too excited about therapy. I just wanted to get back into sparring with two hands. But they insisted, so I was at their mercy.

"PT isn't as bad as you think."

"Mhm." I kept my eyes glued on the next match because I didn't really want to discuss the merits of physical therapy today. I had already heard it from the doctor at the last checkup. "Are you going on furlough this weekend?" I asked, to change the subject. The pack members were headed into the city again and our punishments had been lifted.

I was looking forward to finding someone to let out this pent-up sexual tension with.

"Nah. I got nothing out there." She sighed and leaned against the wall, stretching her legs out in front of her.

"What about your friends?" My gaze moved from the action on the mats to her.

"What friends?" She raised her eyebrows at me. "It's not like I have my pack here with me." She sneered.

I met her gaze, trying to recall any time she was with anyone but me and the pack, and I couldn't. If she wasn't with us, she was alone. My sudden compassion must have shown on my face because she stiffened next to me.

"Don't look at me like you feel sorry for me," she hissed under her breath and crossed her arms.

I reschooled my features and shrugged. "To each his own." I pretended not to care but that sour taste of pity still laced my mouth. I had always been around others and had the pick of who to hang out with if I chose. I couldn't imagine not having the pack.

"Did you have friends before..." I trailed off, still watching the action on the floor.

She sighed. "A couple. But they were so caught up in the social circles at my old high school that we lost touch. The state moved me to the city, where there were more resources for us rejects."

I glanced at her.

"Anyway, your pack seems to be the only ones here who I've gotten to know beyond a nod of acknowledgment." She shrugged. "And it's a bit overwhelming at times."

I chuckled. "You don't like being the center of attention?"

"No. I'd rather kick ass and then fade into the woodwork." She glanced back at the group fighting and the teacher yelling out instructions. "So, a quiet weekend will actually be nice. I can catch up on my work and just chill with a good book."

A very large part of me was torn. I needed to offload some of this stress built up inside me because my lack of being able to spar with anyone to get out the aggression in another manner had been stymied by my broken hand. But knowing she was back here alone left me chilled, as if something bad would happen in my absence.

11

I SHIFTED IN THE passenger seat of Johnson's car, trying to get comfortable while I stared out at the passing scenery. The rest of the pack in the back seats of the SUV talked nonstop about what they were going to do once we arrived in the city. Most of it was finding a girl they'd never meet again and doing all the things my wolf wanted to do with Sarah. All the things I needed to do with a stranger, so I didn't break that cardinal rule with my partner.

It was the first weekend Johnson and I were allowed to leave the Monster Defense Academy since we arrived. It was also the first time since I met Sarah that I was farther than a building away, and that did not sit well.

"What's your problem?" Johnson asked under his breath as he glanced at me.

I just shook my head. I couldn't put it into words, but each mile away turned into pins and needles on my nerve endings. The cafeteria had been nearly barren when we grabbed dinner, and Sarah was one of the few left at school this weekend. We had eaten and bid her goodbye on our way out.

When the city came into view, I shifted again as the prickles became almost a siren wail. "I need to go back."

"What?"

"Something's wrong. Either turn around, or stop and I'll get out."

"But..." He waved at the city, probably thinking I was just being fickle because of my feelings for Sarah. Feelings that the rest of the pack were not privy to.

"You can come back. It's only going to eat an hour of your time if you just drop me off at the door."

Silence settled over the car. "What's going on?" Tom asked from the way back.

"I'm not sure. Alarms are going off in my head, like something bad is happening to my partner." I glanced over my shoulder at him and shrugged. "I have to go back."

They all traded glances. It wasn't unheard of for partners to get distress calls from their magical counterparts. They taught us to be aware of those nagging feelings because they were usually on point.

Johnson took a breath and then turned the vehicle into the grass median, narrowly missing a drop-off. He barreled across, and hit the high speed lane on the opposite side of the highway like a seasoned stunt driver, neatly fitting himself between two speeding cars. He weaved in and out of traffic with his foot to the floor and made it back to campus in half the time.

Instead of parking in the student lot, he slid to a stop in front of the school entry and threw the car into park. Taking the keys out, he nodded at the door. I was already halfway out of the car when the rest of the doors opened and the pack piled out, following my lead.

Desperation clawed at my insides as I nearly ripped the front door off its hinges and ran to the nearest stairwell in the girl's dorm. We pounded up the stairs, sounding more like an earthquake than six men.

My heart hammered in my chest, and the noises coming from inside her room sent a rash of fury through me. I didn't even try Sarah's doorknob. Instead, I lifted my foot and slammed it right next to the locking mechanism, shattering it and throwing the door wide.

Three witches had her pinned face-first to the wall. An array of weapons lay on the floor, and at least one of them had blood on the blade. Her shirt hung in tatters. What made me shift into wolf form was the fact her pants were being pulled down by the asshole standing behind her, who already had his down around his ankles.

The clang of the cast preceded my launch into the air. He didn't even finish his turn toward me and was just registering the shock of our entry when I relieved him of his head. It rolled across the floor and his body fell under my weight.

The shock of the decapitated witch left the other two frozen in fear, with their eyes wide enough to nearly pop from their heads.

I turned on them with my teeth bared and the taste of blood filling my mouth. More than my growls filled the room, too, as my pack fanned out in the small space, pinning them in place. Sarah twisted her wrist free from a witch's grip and a wicked-looking knife appeared in her hand. She speared it right through the bastard's throat with a growl equal to mine.

His last gurgling breaths left us with one asshole to contend with.

That remaining witch let go of Sarah and put his hands up, radiating enough fear to make me want to slowly tear him to shreds just to enjoy his screams.

"What's going on here?"

A stern voice from behind us made all eyes swivel to the door, except mine. Mrs. Kemper, the women's dorm supervisor, gasped from the doorway.

I guess it took her brain a moment to recognize two dead bodies. But it didn't dissuade me from the last blubbering witch. That asshole pointed at Sarah as if this had been her fault. I bared my teeth and every muscle clenched as I readied myself to rid the world of another would-be rapist.

Sarah's movement shifted my gaze, and I glanced at her as she pulled her pants back up with hands that trembled. Even her breathing rasped in unsteady pulls of air as if she held back the tears that I knew had to be there.

"They were attempting to rape my alpha's partner when we came in," Johnson's human voice announced with the same feral fury coursing through me. "He felt her distress, and we came back as fast as possible."

Sarah's gaze shot to mine, her eyes widening a little. A tear escaped the corner, sliding down her face.

That tear cut deeper than I expected, and I focused on the last witch. My wolf demanded retribution. I launched, and my jaws clamped down on his throat as my paws hit him in the chest, knocking him into the wall with a bang.

"Stop!" Mrs. Kemper yelled.

"Armor," Sarah commanded at the same time.

My pelt became heavier just as the witch swung a blade at my side. I expected pain, but metal clanged against metal, and I tore to the side, ripping his throat out before jumping away from the fountain of blood pouring out of the wound.

He slowly dropped to his knees. The knife dropped from his grip, and then he fell face-first into the growing puddle of blood. His last breath hissed from his torn throat.

Sarah stood in the middle of what seemed to be the only dry spot now. Her cheek had a black-and-blue mark on it. As she turned, I caught sight of one of her breasts through the torn shirt. A crescent-shaped bloody mark stood out where one of the bastards dug his nail into her skin. There were other scrapes and bruises on her, but that bloody crescent in the side of her breast pushed my wolf beyond reason.

I attacked the dead corpse, shaking it with all the fury filling me. My snarls carried over the room and my pack shifted into human form, staring at my display of wrath.

Even the teacher backed up.

When the rage finally peeled back a notch or two, I dropped the dead carcass and stepped back, panting.

Mrs. Kemper asked, "Is this true? Were they..." She couldn't seem to finish the sentence, as if the thought was so heinous that even she couldn't fathom it.

Sarah nodded. "Yes. If Robby and his pack hadn't come back..." She visibly shuddered and kept her gaze lowered. She paled as her eyes bounced around the gore streaking her floor.

I glanced at my pack. They all stood in human form with their hands shading their privates. I crossed behind them to the bed and shifted; the metal armor that had saved my wolf from the witch's knife clanged on the ground. I grabbed Sarah's throw blanket and wrapped it around my waist, tying the ends together so it wouldn't fall off, before I turned to my shaking partner.

I crossed to her. My stomach turned at the sensation of warm blood sliding between my toes, but I ignored it. She needed me more than I needed physical comforts. I just pulled her into my arms. "I'm sorry we didn't get here sooner," I whispered.

She nodded against my chest. "You're shaking." She glanced up at me.

"I've never killed anything but game before," I said.

"You will need to go before the academy board for this," Mrs. Kemper said.

I turned, and Mrs. Kemper's incessant blinking chilled me. Her gaze wasn't on me. It was on Sarah, as if all this were somehow her fault.

"I'm sure they will understand my actions," I said, owning my murderous rage.

Her gaze bounced to me, still fluttering her eyelids as though she couldn't comprehend what she was seeing. "I, um, I need to lock you both up until, um, until Monday when the chancellor gets back."

"Can we at least clean off the blood and change clothes?" I asked.

She shook her head. "No. And you boys need to go to your dorm rooms. The chancellor will want to speak with you as well." She pointed out to the hallway and her gaze traveled over the room. Her cheeks paled, and she looked up at us. "Come now, until we can figure out what happened here."

I tightened my jaw.

"It's okay," Sarah whispered against me.

"The hell it is," I barked. "You were attacked and overpowered with the intent to do harm. They deserved the death they got." The snarl in my voice was back. "And this wench somehow thinks that is your fault." I glared at Mrs. Kemper. "It isn't right." I pressed my lips together. "And my father is going to hear about this." I hated pulling that card, but it had the desired effect.

Mrs. Kemper recoiled. "I'm just following protocol." She pointed toward the hall. "We need to secure the crime scene." She waved us out of the room. She closed the door behind us and took each of our arms, leading us down to an area of the school we had never ventured. A trio of cells sat side by side; she opened the first door and pushed me inside, clanging the door closed.

I reached out and hissed as my hands touched the bars. "Silver?" I snapped.

She nodded and shoved Sarah a little more roughly than necessary into the cell beside me. She slammed the cell door closed and stepped back, smoothing out her shirt. "I'll have one of the medical staff come down and take a look at you." This time her voice held a small bit of compassion. "I'm sorry. This is protocol," she added and scurried out of here.

Sarah sat down on the barren mattress and hugged herself. Her teeth started to chatter, so I undid her blanket and reached my hand through the bars, careful not to touch the silver.

"Here. Just as long as you promise not to gawk."

She stared at my hand. "Your cast is gone." She took the blanket and looked away, wrapping it around herself before she sat back down.

"It's probably on your dorm room floor." I sat and placed the pillow over my lap before I flexed my hand open and closed. The shift finished the healing process, like it always does. I scratched the dry skin on my wrist and leaned my head on the concrete wall behind me.

My wolf berated me. *If I had marked her, none of this would have happened.*

I huffed at him. *Yeah, none of this would have happened because she would be dead.*

"Are you okay?" she asked softly.

I looked over at her, realizing she'd been studying me. With an offered smile, I nodded. "I'm sure the fact I killed those guys will hit at some point, but as of right now, I don't have a single regret."

"You didn't kill them all." She glanced down at her hands, one of which was still streaked with blood.

"They deserved it."

She raised her gaze, as if maybe they didn't deserve to die for their transgressions.

"You did nothing wrong."

She laughed. "I said hello as I was leaving the library. I guess that's as good as an invite to my room to the graduates."

I shook my head, focusing on them in my mind. They weren't familiar faces. I don't think anyone in our class would fuck with her, knowing how deadly she was in the sparring ring. I slid my gaze at her. "You didn't beat the shit out of them."

She laughed bitterly. "I tried, but their magic had a little more punch than mine." She reached up to her black-and-blue cheek and winced. "Luckily, it didn't work for long on me. I guess their magic usually held down their victims until they exhausted themselves, but it only held me for a few seconds before I broke through it. Unfortunately, those few seconds were enough for them to physically subdue me once they wised up to the fact their magic wouldn't hold me in place." She shuddered. "If I hadn't been able to fight through their charms..."

"I would have walked in on a whole lot more, and your entire room would be painted with bits of them." I gripped the pillow hard enough for my fingernails to tear into the fabric.

She nodded.

I let her words sink in. "So, they've done that before."

"They bragged about what they were going to do. And that they'd done it to enough lower-level witches over the years to have notches all the way down their bedposts." She cleared her throat and spit into the sink near her. Her aim was impressive. When her gaze slashed back to mine, it was filled with that fire I was used to. Her lips tilted into a dark grin. "I was able to weasel out a name of one of their victims, but it wasn't one I recognized. I figured I'd need someone else to validate my story because I had every intention of killing them. I just didn't know if it would be before or after."

"I felt your... anxiety."

"That's a good word for it."

"You know what I mean."

"I'm glad. I wasn't purposely transmitting, though."

I took a deep breath. Usually, partners send out a mental transmission in times of stress. What she didn't know was that fated mates have a stronger connection than MDA partners did, even when they weren't mated. And I was living with those signals every day. I seemed to be able to read her every mood pretty damn accurately because of the bond.

Good Lord, what the hell would this connection be like if I actually claimed her? I slid my gaze to hers and shrugged. "I don't know what to tell you. I felt your unease and when it turned to alarm, I told Johnson to either stop the car or turn around."

"Thank you." She wrapped the blanket tighter around her shoulders.

"You'd do the same if I was in trouble."

She snorted a laugh and met my gaze. "I don't think I'm physically capable of decapitating someone with the snap of my jaws."

I grinned and stared at the floor.

"But yes. I'd kill to protect you."

Her soft admission nearly released my wolf, but I took a deep breath and just nodded my acknowledgment. "Think you could do that magic thing so I'm not sitting here naked?"

"Unfortunately, I can't. I tried already. We're both stuck in what we've got on until someone comes and lets us out."

"Fan-fucking-tastic," I muttered, and stretched out on the cot with the pillow still draped over my lap.

"How much trouble do you think we're in?"

I stared at the ceiling and chewed on my lip before I tilted my head back to look at her. "You have nothing to worry about." I would see to that. What those assholes tried to do and apparently had done to others was no better than any of the monsters they were training us to hunt, and they should get the same capital punishment for their vile deeds.

12

TURNED OUT WE HAD to stay in those cells for longer than I cared for without a change of clothes or the opportunity to wash the blood off. Saturday came without so much as a crumb of food or anyone coming down. No medical staff to check out Sarah and no food and not even a jug of clean water.

I didn't even know what time it was, but I knew we had been in these cells for at least twelve hours.

"You'd think they'd at least bring us breakfast," I muttered, glaring at the bright hallway outside of the dim cells.

"Can you look the other way?" she asked.

I raised an eyebrow and looked at the wall instead of at her. The sound of a bladder releasing into a toilet echoed on the walls. Her sigh of relief made me smile. I glanced at the toilet in the corner of my cell. The sink turned on and ran, and then after the water turned off, I waited until the sound of mattress springs creaked before I reacted.

"My turn." I stood, dropping the pillow onto the bed. I wasn't as modest as she was. If she looked, she'd see my bare ass. I relieved myself, washed my hands, and then took a few handfuls of water from the faucet. It left a metallic taste as if these pipes hadn't been used in ages. I forced a couple of breaths before I returned to the mattress. I replaced the pillow over my lap and stretched out.

Saturday blurred as we waited for someone to come by.

"Do you think they forgot about us?" I asked as my stomach groaned again. At least it was just noise right now. I didn't look forward to another day of being incommunicado with my pack. Instead of dwelling on our situation, I sat up and crossed to the sink. At least we had water. I leaned over so my mouth was as close to under the faucet as possible and turned on the cold water, swallowing gulp after gulp to help with the stomach pangs.

"I don't know." Sarah lay curled up on her side on the cot. "But we can go a week or two with just water." She sent me a morbid smile.

Well, no one came Saturday either and by Sunday morning, my stomach growl had dropped into a category that rivaled my feral growl. My face had stubble growing and it itched like hell. The dried blood was flaking in places, and I could tell I smelled less like a man and more like an animal.

Sarah wasn't much better, except she still had that citrusy scent that made her rankness more palatable.

My stomach groaned, and she giggled.

I rolled onto my side and adjusted the pillow, glancing at her through the bars. "You find my stomach growling funny?" I pressed my lips together against a smile.

"It's obnoxious."

"Being locked up here for two nights is obnoxious," I muttered under my breath as my stomach was nearly eating itself.

"Did you get any sleep?" she asked through a yawn.

I nearly laughed out loud. With her this close to me, I couldn't relax enough to sleep, not with her readjusting her position so often that I just wanted to break through the bars and hold her and chase her nightmares away.

"Not really," I answered and glanced back. "You snore."

The hallway door creaked open, and I sat up.

Johnson came into the hall, carrying a stack of my clothes. Mr. Fritz, the men's dorm supervisor who had initially showed me to my room on the first day, flanked Johnson on one side and Mrs. Kemper on the other. Johnson didn't quite meet our gazes. It was as if he had been told not to engage.

My gaze bypassed Johnson's and landed on Mrs. Kemper. "What the hell? You were supposed to send one of the medical techs to check her out. And what's with not sending us food?"

Mr. Fritz sneered at me and then slashed a glare at Sarah. Mrs. Kemper couldn't meet either of our stares.

"I figured you needed clothes and..." Johnson started but Mr. Fritz cleared his throat. Johnson glared at him. "Neither of them did anything wrong," he snapped and the muscles in his arms tightened under his shirt like he were getting ready to take a swing.

If Johnson continued, he'd end up in a cell, too. "Thanks for the clothes." I started to get up.

"Stay where you are," Mr. Fritz snapped.

I sat back down with the pillow over my privates.

Mrs. Kemper unlocked the cell and waved for Johnson to enter with the stash of clothing. "Just put it on the floor and then come out."

"Fine," Johnson muttered under his breath and stepped in far enough to clear the door. He put the clothing down and exited just as quickly. His frustration radiated from him. Even without my heightened senses, it was visible in the scowl on his face and the tenseness in his muscles. As they walked out, he glanced my way and the trepidation in that one look clenched my stomach.

I retrieved the clothes, and as I pulled out the underwear and slid them on, a piece of paper stuck out from between the folds of my jeans. Before I unfolded it, I pulled my jeans on and slipped one of the T-shirts over my head. The fact he had given me an extra shirt struck me as odd.

I unfolded the note and read the first line. "Johnson thought you might like a shirt, too." I held the extra T-shirt out to her, careful not to touch the bars.

"That was nice of him." She took the cloth and turned away from me to slip off her shredded shirt, replacing it with my oversized top.

It took me a second to tear my eyes away from her and back to the note. They were planning to crucify both of us.

I huffed. Their lack of attention to us in any form told me enough, but Johnson's note just compounded the truth that this organization was as evil as the monsters we hunted.

"You have that name, right?" I asked her as I read his assessment of what they were charging us with: She lured those men into her room. I killed them out of some jealous rage, per their write-up. The pack would not be allowed to testify on our behalf. I closed my eyes and nearly crumpled the paper.

"Yes."

"Do you think anyone else at the school has been attacked?" I glanced at her. The entire school would be witness to this farce, and if we had allies in the audience, I needed to know.

She chewed her lip and nodded. "I think at least one has from what they were saying. But I'm not sure. Why?"

I handed her Johnson's note.

As she read it, her cheeks turned red and I swear, for a moment fire blazed in her eyes. "Is he kidding?" Her gaze slashed to mine.

I shook my head. "We're going to need others to validate your story."

She looked at the paper in her hand again. "Isn't your father on the board?"

"Yep," I said. "But I don't think it'll matter unless we can prove they were repeat rapists."

Sarah crumpled the paper and shot it into the toilet, cursing under her breath. She flushed the toilet and then threw herself on the cot.

"Those assholes promised me I'd hang if I said anything," she muttered and met my gaze.

"That's not happening." I would make certain it didn't, because I would spill a whole lot of MDA blood if they tried. And I wouldn't be alone. My pack would back me. It would be an outright war.

Sarah slung her arm over her eyes and sighed.

We went another restless night without food. In the morning, the door creaked open, and Mr. Fritz and Mrs. Kemper approached our cells with frowns of disgust.

Not a word was said. They just opened the doors and waited until we stepped out. Mrs. Kemper led the way, and Mr. Fritz took the position in back of us. It felt like walking the green mile as we were marched through the halls into the cafeteria. No food was present. Only a table with two chairs faced the raised stage. On the raised platform in front of us, the administrators of the academy, along with the teachers, sat. In the center was my father.

I held one of the chairs for Sarah and then took my seat next to her. My father's dark stare was enough to make me want to fidget, but I remained stoic, with my hands folded before me. I didn't break eye contact with him, either. It was my silent challenge to this ludicrous display.

When the students filed in, lining the walls and gathering behind us, my father broke his gaze and surveyed the crowd.

I glanced at Sarah, but she had her hands clenched in her lap; she stared at the table, her face pale enough to give me pause. That was when I felt the force of her terror. I had been so consumed with staring down my father that I blocked everything else. And her terror felt like a swarm of bees attacking me. I took a breath and glared out at those in charge. I would annihilate them if they tried to harm her.

One of the administrators cleared her throat, and her face pinched in distaste as she looked at us. I had only seen her in attendance at orientation, so I didn't have a clue what her name was. The whispering in the auditorium died down to a hush.

"We are gathered today to pass judgment on these two students. One who seduced three graduates and the other who killed them in a jealous rage." She waved at us.

My pack scoffed in unison.

"There will be no interruptions from the crowd!" she snarled.

"So, the academy endorses rape." I projected my voice so it reached every single ear in the room. I leaned back in the seat, crossing my arms, displaying the dried blood still streaking my skin.

She blinked at me and pointed a gnarled finger in my direction. "Silence!"

I slammed my hand on the table and stood. "I will not be silent. Those thugs attacked *my* partner. And they've done this before. She was not the first. And if they had succeeded, she wouldn't be the last. Those bastards deserved a slow and painful death, and not the quick work I made of them."

Her mouth dropped.

Sarah stared up at me with wide eyes, as if my outburst wasn't warranted.

"Son..." my father started.

"You condone what was done?" I snarled, glaring at him. "You condone witches controlling their victims? Making them do vile things just for their twisted enjoyment?" I slung the words like weapons and turned toward the crowd, scanning them. Two female witches looked at the ground, just as pale as Sarah. My anger flared even more, and I glanced back at our judge and jury.

I straightened my spine. "And you would condemn an innocent for this?" I felt power swell inside me as the alpha in my wolf bristled. The wolves around me and on the stage seemed to shrink in on themselves. Even my father had a moment where he seemed to be cowering. "You. Will. Not." The power in my voice rolled over the entire room. Even some of the witches seemed to roll into themselves against the power I projected with those three words.

"You are not in the position to make demands," my father said through clenched teeth, as if denying my alpha order.

I smiled. "I am the alpha here." I stabbed my finger on the table. "I stand for what is right for *my* pack, and my pack includes witches and wolves from all over, standing obediently in attendance behind me. If it was one of your pack members who was assaulted, you wouldn't bat an eye at my swift justice. Well, it was *my* pack member who these three assholes assaulted." I turned and pointed to the two other witches who still shielded their eyes, and then waved at Sarah. "And they did nothing but nod a hello in the library when their partners were not here to protect them."

"But they were strong mages," the pinched-faced woman whined, as if that gave them a pass to violate anyone.

"I don't give a fuck who they were. They used their magic to sexually assault young witches. That makes them a target of this agency that you are training us all for. Dark magic is prohibited." I took a breath and glanced at Sarah. "And if you still choose to condemn her, you condemn me. I will not stand by and let you kill an innocent because of some archaic rules of engagement that do not apply to this situation. In other words, you will have to go through me to get to my partner. And I'll take as many of you down with me as I possibly can." I stared down my father, putting the stakes out on the table.

"She's a witch."

"She's part of *my* pack." I slapped my palm on my chest. "And I protect *my* pack. Had I known this was happening, I would have annihilated the three rapists before last night. They were the abominations, not the women who fell victim to their trickery."

Every eye in the room was on me. Admiration flowed in waves from the student body surrounding us, and animosity charged from the board in front of us, as if I should have remained quiet and subdued like a good student.

"How did you hold them off long enough for your partner to return?" one of the witches behind me asked in a voice that held devastation. Her blonde hair was tucked behind her ears, and she had stepped to the front of the crowd, her eyes imploring Sarah for an answer. She was partner to Hannah, a member of my hometown pack.

Sarah turned and shrugged, speaking for the first time since this farce of a trial began. "It was a struggle, but I was able to break through their bitter magic every time they slung it at me."

Hannah stepped out of the crowd and focused on her partner. "They assaulted you?"

A tear slid down the girl's face, and she nodded.

"Why didn't you tell me?" Hannah asked soft enough that the board didn't hear her, but both Sarah and I did, and we exchanged a glance. The focus and care Hannah showed displayed exactly what partners were supposed to do for each other.

"Because those assholes told her they would see to it that she was executed if she breathed a word to anyone." Sarah swallowed and looked at the board, all passing judgment on us. "It was the same threat they tried to impress on me as I fought them off and mentally sent an SOS to my partner."

"You weren't the only ones." A second witch with dark hair hanging in her face stepped forward; a wolf from another pack snarled at the board and then focused on her emotionally wounded partner.

A third and fourth student stepped forward, adding to our defense. That made one witch assaulted for every weekend since the furloughs started. My stomach clenched. I turned my anger toward the front of the room. How long had they *allowed* this shit to go on?

I leaned forward on the table, reining in my furious wolf. "Are you going to condemn *my* pack?"

In that one growling sentence, I became the leader of the entire school. The shift of emotions in the room altered in our favor. Not only did I have the support of my pack members who had witnessed the atrocity, but the rest of the wolves and witches stood with us.

There would be brutal bloodshed if the board condemned us now.

13

MY FATHER'S GAZE SCANNED over the crowd. "Mrs. Wyman, perhaps we should discuss this with the accused in private."

At least the bastard was smart enough to read the room correctly.

The pinched-faced woman glared at him and then looked at me. "And what of the charges of jealousy, Mr. Young?"

I laughed and traded a heated look with my father before meeting her gaze. "I protected my partner. If doing what we're taught at this academy is considered jealousy, then that's truly fucked up. I would have reacted just as violently had I walked in on those assholes abusing *any* of the women in this room, including you." I pointed my finger at her. "My mother taught me right from wrong and ingrained in me a strong sense of swift justice. I act when I witness evil, ma'am."

My father's gaze swept over me as if he saw me for the first time. As if he had just witnessed me level every alpha in the region on the mat. I shocked him with my conviction.

Too bad he didn't think it was real. Granted, Sarah *was* my true mate and seeing what they were trying to do drove my wolf over the brink of reason, but it had nothing to do with jealousy. It had everything to do with rage. Rage regarding the audacity of those assholes to think they had a right to touch Sarah without her consent.

When my father's chest swelled with pride, I narrowed my eyes at him. He wasn't the one who taught me how to respond to evil. All the credit on that went to my mother.

"You have not answered my question. Are you condemning *my* pack?" I asked again. I wasn't backing down, not with our lives in the crosshairs.

Johnson stepped next to me, followed by the rest of my hometown pack. Then the rest of the student body pressed forward, forming a solid line around us, and we severely outnumbered the board.

Sarah slid her chair back and stood up as well, adding to our display of unity.

Mrs. Wyman glanced around at her peers, getting consistent head shakes as she met each member's gaze. She faced forward and folded her hands in front of her as she scanned all of us. She finally looked at me.

"No, Mr. Young. We are not going to condemn your pack today. But we will be watching you and Miss Stone. If there is any more trouble, you two will be facing harsher punishments than just a few nights in lockup."

"Thank you, ma'am. Now if you would excuse us, we need to go clean up."

I turned without waiting for any response. The crowd parted, and we marched out of the cafeteria, and separated at the outer doors. Sarah headed back toward her room, and I to mine.

Johnson caught up with me just as I stepped into the room.

"Thanks for the heads-up." I closed the door behind me.

"No problem. From what I gathered, they were aiming to have Sarah killed. It made no fucking sense to me, and you needed to know." He stretched out on his bed.

I stripped out of the clothes and headed for the shower to scrub the dried blood off me, but a knock on the door made me pause. I grabbed the towel off the back of the bathroom door, wrapped it around me, and answered the door.

Sarah stood in the hall, looking lost. Her eyes widened as they took in my bare chest, and then she met my gaze.

"Um. My room is still..." She licked her lips and shifted from foot to foot. "Can I use your shower?"

"They haven't cleaned up your room?" I stepped back, waving her into our quarters.

"No. They haven't even removed the bodies." Her face turned a shade paler.

"Jesus." I grabbed the clothes that Johnson had brought to me in the jail cell and stepped into the bathroom, redressing myself. When I entered the room again, I said, "I'll clean up my mess." After all, I was the one who shredded the shit out of two humans. "You are welcome to use our shower." I nodded toward the bathroom.

She looked at the bathroom and then at me, as if debating. "You weren't the only one who killed." She took a deep breath and let it out slowly. "I'll help you, but I can't guarantee I won't throw up."

I smiled. I was glad I didn't have anything in my stomach. "I might, too," I admitted. The thought of cleaning up human remains left a sour taste in my mouth, but I wasn't going to leave her to do it alone.

"Do you want me there?" Johnson asked.

Sarah looked at him and shook her head. "You don't need to be there."

"More hands to help." He raised his hands, waving his fingers.

That pulled a smile onto Sarah's face. "If you want to clean up blood and guts, then I guess you're welcome to join."

"Not that I want to, but we were all there, so I'm willing to dispose of the garbage, too."

I couldn't tell whether Johnson was flirting with Sarah or not, but the idea of help wasn't one I was going to turn down. We stepped into the hall and headed toward the girl's dorm. When we got to Sarah's floor, the four women who had been assaulted were hanging around the door to Sarah's room. As we approached, they turned to us.

We stopped in front of them.

"I'm sorry for calling you out," I said before any of them could speak.

Hannah's partner gave me an uneasy smile. "Thank you for stopping them."

I extended my hand. "Robby Young."

"Heddie Thompson." She shook my hand.

"I'm sorry that we didn't know to stop them before they attacked you," Sarah said. "We would have filleted their asses sooner had we known." She swung her door open to the carnage.

I might not have been so insensitive, but none of the girls gasped or shied away from the bloody scene. A satisfied smile actually appeared on Heddie's lips as she surveyed the damage.

Then Heddie looked at me and Johnson. "Thank you."

"No problem at all. As I said in that farce of a tribunal, everyone here is part of my pack and as such, it's my duty to protect you from harm." I shuffled my feet and looked in at what I had done in my rage. "I'm sorry I failed you," I added, looking back at the four girls. I really should have known what was going on.

"No one knew. We didn't even know among ourselves." She waved at the other three witches who hadn't been introduced. "If they had assaulted a wolf, you would have known."

"True." I couldn't argue with her. Wolves carried a stronger bond of silent communication.

"I'm still trying to figure out how your partner was able to give you a heads-up that something was wrong," Heddie mumbled under her breath as her gaze jumped between me and Sarah.

"I guess we're on the same...wavelength." Sarah shrugged. "I'm just glad I was able to break their spells."

Heddie's brow creased. "How?"

Sarah glanced in the room and sighed. "Sheer force of will."

"I was terrified. I couldn't even think straight," Heddie said.

"Yeah, well, I was pissed and plotting their deaths." With that, Sarah stepped into the room. "I don't even know where to begin."

"Disposing of the bodies might be a good start," I said from behind her as I surveyed the carnage. "Damn," I whispered at the extent of blood and gore coating the room.

Sarah looked back at me. "You were truly terrifying in action."

I let out a laugh, but it wasn't quite my natural bust-a-gut laugh. This one held the raw nerves now playing across my skin at what was left of the last body. The first two would be easier to pick up. But the last one was in pieces. I glanced up at the ceiling; there were even splatters of blood and bits of skin and bone stuck on the cinderblocks above us.

"Do you have garbage bags and rags and cleaning solution?" I asked.

"A mop and a bucket?" Johnson piped in.

"Cleaning gloves?" Heddie said from behind us.

I turned. The four witches hadn't left. They stood behind us, as if they intended to help.

"You really don't need to help," Sarah echoed my thoughts. "We've got this."

Heddie glanced at Sarah and around the room. "I can't get rid of it, but I can concentrate the mess into a single pile."

We all turned and looked at her. Sarah's eyebrows probably mimicked mine.

"I can control matter," she said.

I did recall things moving at her opponents when she fought in the gym. Even Hannah had to dodge a projected missile coming for her in the ring.

"Telekinetic?" Sarah nodded, as if she recalled the same things. Sarah had fought her, too. But Sarah was unbeatable in the ring, even with magic coming at her in all forms. Which was probably why she was able to break through these assholes' magic. She had proved she had that skill time and time again in sparring matches.

Heddie nodded and looked up at the splatters on the ceiling. A crease appeared between her eyes, and she splayed her hand out, moving it slowly toward the wall, where more splatters of blood covered the concrete blocks. The mess followed her hand, rolling away and leaving the cinderblock clean. It looked like a giant had wiped away the blood and guts in one stroke of a sponge. Heddie continued, pulling the grime from the walls and gathering it all into a pile on the floor.

Sarah's ceiling, walls, and furniture were clean when Heddie finished. But the witch looked as though she hadn't slept in days from the effort.

"Thank you." Sarah marveled at the newly sparkling room. The floor was another story, but the linoleum would clean easily with a mop and bucket once we removed the bodies. "You should go get some rest or something to eat," she added.

Heddie and the others left us to finish cleaning up.

Sarah conjured up large, thick garbage bags like the ones used for construction garbage, along with shovels and three buckets of bleach-smelling liquid with mops.

A throat cleared from behind us, and we turned.

My father stood in the doorway, along with Mrs. Kemper.

"We are here to collect the bodies," Mrs. Kemper said.

I glared at her. "And you couldn't do it before that farce of a trial?" I growled.

"Easy, son." My father tried to appease me.

All it did was aggravate me more. "Fuck you," I snapped. He stood by the rest of the board. He wouldn't have intervened if they had convicted us. He would prefer to keep his station in the agency than support his son.

"Robby," Sarah said sternly.

Johnson actually put his hand on my shoulder and shook his head.

My father glared at Sarah. "I don't need you interjecting in my conversation with my son."

"She can interject her thoughts into any conversation that I'm having," I snarled and pushed with my alpha powers. "She is my partner and as such, you will not disrespect her or anyone else in my pack."

My father growled in response.

"We were not allowed to disrupt the room until a verdict was issued," Mrs. Kemper said while she uncontrollably wrung her hands. "Please step out while we take care of this."

"Fine." I stormed past, brushing my shoulder against his and knocking him back a step on purpose. Sarah and Johnson followed me out. Three men with insignias from the coroner's office stood outside with a cart piled with body bags.

They replaced us in the room.

My father stepped out in the hall and leveled a stare at me that was supposed to make me fidget, but I crossed my arms and pressed my lips together against the flurry of derogatory words that wanted to slip free.

"I wouldn't have let them harm you," he said softly.

"But you sure as shit would have let my partner hang." I nodded toward Sarah as my head pulsed with anger.

His gaze sharpened. "I could not influence the board's decision."

"Bullshit," I snarled and turned, walking away. If I stayed, I'd throw a punch.

A hand caught my shoulder and I tensed, spinning back, thinking it was my father, but Sarah stood there instead. She poked me in the chest hard.

"He's your father, and he's here. He could be gone tomorrow, so you have to give him some slack."

I knew she was coming from a place where neither parent was here, and she saw things differently than I did. *If she knew what he had done, would she still be coming to his defense?* But I wasn't about to spill that secret. Especially if she struggled with the electricity between us as much as I did, because it was always there for me.

"He's a bastard who didn't lift a finger to save us."

She blinked up at me. "He's still your father."

I closed my eyes and hung my head. A moment later, the squeak of the cart drew my eyes open. The coroner staff pushed the cart out the door, loaded with three body bags.

"We'll talk later," my father said from where he stood.

I gave a nod without looking at him. I was sure during winter break I'd hear more than an earful. But for now, we still had the rest of the semester to get through, which wouldn't be easy with the added scrutiny.

14

THE NEXT FEW WEEKS were uneventful. It was as if my declaration in front of the board had elevated me to the untouchable realm. It was irritating, especially because I was back in the sparring ring and no one but Sarah would give me their best. Even Johnson pulled his punches, as if going at me at full capacity was some sort of sin.

"What the fuck, man," I grumbled and slammed the door to our room.

"Dude, you're the alpha. No one wants to challenge you."

"How the hell am I supposed to get better at fighting if no one will actually give me their best?"

"Your partner does. She's fucking fearless."

He nailed it dead-on. Sarah was fearless. And angry. And smart. A challenge to me in every conceivable way. She could outwit and outmaneuver me in the ring unless I turned wolf, and then she still bested me most of the time. But the times I took her to the mat were my favorite. It gave me a second with her underneath me, with her eyes ablaze and her breath heaving. Thankfully, I was in wolf form when that happened, but it still took everything not to claim her in those moments.

"That she is," I muttered. Instead of arguing with Johnson, I stripped and stepped into the shower, letting the warm water wash the sweat off my under-utilized muscles. I was not looking forward to winter break. I had obligations at home with the job I had at the local dive, waiting tables. I planned to give notice before I came back, because in the spring, we'd become full-fledged agents and get assigned to wherever the hell they wanted to place us.

I was hoping for somewhere up north in mountain country, but with my luck lately, it would probably be at headquarters in the city, which didn't thrill me. I liked the countryside, where I could shift and just run until my muscles gave out. Although, the alternative would likely be in my father's office, and that would be worse than death. Having my old man hanging over my shoulder every second of every day would drive me batshit.

Plus, not seeing Sarah on a daily basis was going to be rough. Regardless of the situation, seeing her was the highlight of my day.

My stomach growled as I toweled off and dressed. I figured if I could stretch out the evening somehow, I wouldn't have to pile into Johnson's car afterward and head into the lion's den.

I stepped out of the bathroom and scanned my things. Johnson had his duffel bag stuffed for the trek home, but I was only going to bring my dirty laundry home. I didn't need to carry it back and forth if I didn't have to. I stuffed my duffel with my towels and the clothing in my laundry basket while Johnson cleaned up.

I didn't wait for Johnson. I wanted as much time with Sarah before he carted me off for the winter break, and like the first day, we were both early and the doors hadn't opened yet.

"Hiding from everyone?" she asked as she slid onto the bench.

I sat and nodded. "I'm not looking forward to going home, either."

She snorted a laugh. "Well, I'll be here if you need me."

I raised an eyebrow.

"Where am I going to go?" She leveled a look as though I had actually spoken.

I had forgotten that she was in state care outside of these walls. "If you need me, just text and I'll be here as fast as I can. Or call like you did before." I gave her a halfhearted smile, praying she wouldn't have to send out a mental SOS again. I wouldn't be able to get back here as fast as I had that night.

She paled a fraction and nodded. "Let's hope I don't need to. But I'll text you to death because I'm sure I'm going to be bored senseless here."

Sarah was not one to sit idle. Ever. Even studying in the library, she had to jump up and go find this book or that book to answer her questions. I don't think I've ever seen her sit down for more than ten minutes at a time, unless we were eating. She was worse than I was, with energy to burn.

"If I don't answer, don't think I'm ignoring you. I'm probably working."

"You've still got a job at home?"

"Yes. But I need to give my notice because I won't be going back after break."

"What do you do?"

"Wait tables. The pay is shit, but the tips are pretty good."

She stared at me and shook her head. "I can't see you waiting tables."

I stretched my left arm out. "I can balance more plates on my arm than anyone else in town. And I've never dropped any of them." I grinned. "Ever."

"Well, you just jinxed yourself." She pointed at me just as the locks on the cafeteria doors clicked and the staff pushed the doors open.

"We'll see about that." I stood and waved for her to go first. She made a beeline to the buffet, and we had our plates overflowing before any of the other students stepped into the cafeteria.

The cafeteria filled quickly as we scarfed down our food, sitting in the same end seats we had become accustomed to. The pack and their partners filled up the rest of the table along with the witches who helped us clean Sarah's room.

The seat next to Sarah was now reserved for Hannah, and Johnson always sat to my right no matter where we seemed to be. Everyone nodded at me as they passed, and frankly, outside of the ring, I liked the show of respect. If only I could get them all to understand that their respect should translate into giving me their all when we sparred.

Dinner flew by too fast, and Johnson nudged me with his elbow. I gave him a look, and he tapped his watch.

"I know. I'm just not thrilled at the prospect of going home," I muttered, and Sarah raised her eyebrow from across the table. I stood with my tray and reached for hers.

"I got it. You don't have to clear my tray." She smiled up at me as she held her side of the cheap plastic so I couldn't just swipe it off the table. "I might go for a little more of the apple crisp anyway." She nodded to the dessert section and the abundance of apple crisp still sitting there.

"It doesn't seem like it's that good." I still eyed the dessert, but now I could smell it above all other scents, and it did trigger my mouth to water.

"Stop stalling. Go home and make amends with your dad."

Her tone didn't give me any choice.

I rolled my eyes and headed out, dumping my tray in the tray caddie before Johnson and I went to grab our bags.

I stretched out in the front seat and stared out the window as Johnson drove. This time it was just the two of us, and he had the sense to keep quiet. The closer we came to home, the more my mood worsened.

"It's not going to be as bad as you think," Johnson said.

I scoffed at him. My father was going to beat the crap out of me for my indiscretions. I'd be sporting bruises for weeks from the whupping that was sure to greet me the minute I stepped through the door. After all, I had challenged the alpha.

15

I WAS NOT WRONG to be wary of home. Johnson stopped in front of the dark mansion I had left four months ago. The hairs on the back of my neck prickled.

"Thanks for the ride." I grabbed my duffel from the back.

"No problem. I'll see you in a couple days. I think we cross shifts next weekend at Joe's."

"I'll see you then." With a nod, I closed the car door and headed toward my house, digging in my pocket for the house key. I slipped inside and set my bag down. Shoes came off next because, regardless of being a wolf, we were not to track mud into the house. It was something my mother pounded into my head and although she had died almost ten years ago, I still respected her rules.

No sounds hung on the heavy air. Not even the echo of a breath in the house. However, I felt the malevolent anger pressing down on me. Instead of heading into the family room, I grabbed my bag and headed up the stairs to my bedroom.

The moment I stepped into the room, I startled at the figure standing at the window. I hadn't even looked up when I got out of the car; otherwise, I would have seen him. I expected my father in his recliner in the family room, not standing sentry at my window.

For a moment, I was my younger self and all I wanted was an ice cream treat, but I hadn't done my chores and my father said no. I snuck a dollar from his wallet and when I returned home from enjoying the ice cream, he had been standing in the same place wearing that same fiery glare.

But this time, he was not justified in his anger.

I threw my duffel on the floor. "What?" I bellowed at him.

"Don't you use that tone with me." He pointed his finger at me. His sharp canines were on display, which meant he was particularly dangerous.

"I will use whatever tone I please."

He was on me in an instant and slammed me into the wall. "You are not the alpha here," he growled in my face.

"No?" I cocked my head and pushed out the alpha influence like I had at that farce of a trial. I narrowed my eyes at him, but I did not strike out like my clenched hands wanted to. I still honored my mother, and beating the shit out of my father wasn't something she'd be proud of. But I could bend him to my will.

He growled at me and landed the first punch right into my left side.

Air rushed out of my lungs, but I refused to curl over. Hell, I had been hit harder sparring with Sarah. "Back off," I warned.

I parried before his next punch connected, catching him off guard as I deflected his fist, sending it into the wall next to me, and then I spun out of his grip. It was something I had never had the guts to do before. Oh, I was capable, but I was still under his influence, whether I liked it or not.

All that fury that I carried inside since he fucked with my entire life surfaced and I growled, baring my teeth, but I didn't shift into wolf form. My wolf was even more furious at the old man; if I set him free, he would fight to the death.

"Isn't fucking up the rest of my life enough of a punishment? Or would you prefer to bury me?" I glared at him.

My words had the same effect a hefty slap would have. My father reeled back a step and his eyes widened as his jaw dropped. "I would never…"

"Yet you are so willing to beat me." I stayed out of reach. "And take away the one thing that would make me complete."

"She's a witch," he hissed, as if she were a leper instead. "She put you under some sort of spell."

I laughed. "Sarah couldn't cast a spell to save her life. Do you know what her magic is?"

"I don't need to know. She is not a werewolf, and she is trouble."

"She is not trouble. She's fiercer than any wolf in this pack. Fiercer than Mom."

"No one was as fierce as your mother. And yet she still was taken by a blood sucker." His teeth slipped back to human. "I did what I did to protect you."

"Protect me, or your status?" I snapped back, with my fangs still on display. I put my hand up, splaying my fingers out. "Don't answer that. I already know." I ran my hand through my hair, trying to rein in my aggravation. "Coming home was a mistake."

"You have obligations here."

I hated the fact he was right. I couldn't just leave. I had to give some sort of notice to the restaurant, but it was going to be a hell of a lot shorter than originally planned. "Get out of my bedroom," I snapped and pointed at the door. "As soon as my obligations are met, I'm out of here."

"I have someone I want you to meet," he had the audacity to say. "She will make a perfect alpha's mate."

"I'm never agreeing to anyone you decide is a proper mate. I already met my true mate and nothing on this earth is going to sway me any other way. And because of what you did, there will be no heritage to hand down beyond me. I'm the end of the line."

He paled at my words and went to open his mouth.

"It's all your doing." I pointed at him. "This is the consequence of *your* actions." Instead of waiting for him to leave my room, I turned and walked out of the house, shifting the moment I hit the sidewalk. I needed to run until this anger dialed back. Otherwise, I was going to do something colossally stupid. Like challenge the current alpha, which would mean only one of us would walk out of that alive. And although I was angry, I did not want to commit patricide.

THE NEXT DAY, I walked into Joe's and into the office where Maddy sat at the desk, doing the schedule. She looked up and smiled, but it only held for a moment.

"What's up?" she asked with a voice that bordered on concern.

"I'm giving my notice." I moved my weight nervously from foot to foot. I didn't like disappointing Maddy. Not when she had gone out of her way to give me a job despite my father's initial protests against being a lowly waiter.

She looked at the paper in front of her and then back at me. "How long?"

"What's the minimum?" I cringed as I asked. The longer I was at home, the more likely I was going to take a swing at my father.

"Customarily, it's two weeks." She used her hands to smooth out the paper in front of her, scanning the schedule she was making.

I nodded and sighed. I knew that was the usual. But I couldn't fathom being in the same house as my father for that long. Not with the volatility between us right now.

There had to be a way to shorten that timespan. "You wouldn't bend on that, would you?"

She leaned back in her chair. "You have something better lined up?" She pursed her lips, studying me.

"No. But staying will result in bloodshed," I admitted. She had seen me sporting bruises a time or two before and although I brushed them off, I could see the suspicion in her eyes.

Maddy looked down at the schedule in front of her and chewed on her lip. "Think you can get through three days?" She looked up at me. "If so, I can rearrange things so you have longer shifts over the next three days, and then we can call it even. Would that work?"

"Yeah." I gave her a partial smile, knowing her accommodating me might come back to bite her. After all, I was talking about bloodshed with the pack alpha. And I hadn't been given that role yet. I was no longer sure my father would give me that honor, or whether I would eventually have to fight him to the death for it.

16

I ARRIVED HOME FROM my first shift and the house was blissfully empty, so I unwrapped the cheese steak I had brought home from the restaurant and set myself up in front of the television. I found new episodes of a series I had been watching before I went off to the academy and pressed play.

My father came in during the second episode, and it was as if a horde of bees had entered with him. The tension between us ratcheted up so high that the meal I scoffed down started to feel as if I swallowed lead.

Two more full days of work before I could kiss this tension goodbye. Although I was sure it would feel more like years by the time I got on my bike and headed back to school.

"What the hell are you watching?" He glared at me as he settled into his chair with what looked like takeout. Of course, he only had one take out box with him, so if I hadn't brought home my dinner, I would have had to order something from delivery or go without. The cupboards here were pretty barren, as if my father hadn't been hanging out at home much.

"A show." I didn't bother looking over at him either. My phone dinged, and I glanced at it. My first text from Sarah, and I couldn't help the smile that formed. Instead of fishing for how I was dealing with my dad, she jumped right in, telling me about her day.

Apparently, they had her helping out in the kitchen. That's something I couldn't really see her doing, but she promised she'd make us all something when we got back, but to set my expectations, she did make charcoal out of a batch of brownies, so it was an eat-at-your-own-risk situation.

I chuckled under my breath.

"If you're not going to watch this crap, give me the remote," my father growled.

"I am watching it."

"You're texting. That isn't watching the show," he grumbled.

I sent him a look that would have shut anyone else up, but he returned it with the same fierceness.

"I can leave and never come back, you know."

"You aren't eighteen yet."

"Um, yes, I am." I couldn't help the snark in my voice. It happened to be around the same time we got benched at school and I found out about Sarah's parents. My father hadn't even sent a card. But if I really thought about it, he hadn't ever been the one to initiate the celebration. It was always someone else in the pack bringing a cake over.

He blinked and creased his brow, as if he were trying to remember my actual day of birth.

"October, Dad. My birthday was in October." I tossed him the remote and stormed away, making sure my steps were heavy enough to vibrate the floorboards. I walked out into the cold night and pulled out my phone again, rereading Sarah's text, letting the chill of the air cool me down.

Even with anger thrumming in my veins like a high voltage blast, her words soothed the beast inside me, and I took breath after breath, seeing my exhale on the frosty air.

Two days. That's all I needed to endure. That is, if we didn't come to blows.

I started to write a text of the shit going down and deleted it just as fast. I did not want to lay my problems at Sarah's feet. Not when she really had no understanding of the years of constant friction between me and my father. She also had no clue of what the man had done to us. I'm not sure she would be so understanding if she knew he had intentionally sabotaged our future.

I tucked the phone into my pocket and glanced up at the clear, moonless night. The constellations stood out against the black canvas in pins of bright light. This view didn't happen in the city. I circled around the house to our picnic table and stretched out on the cold wooden surface on my back. Every now and then, a satellite would track overhead, crossing the sky in an arc before it disappeared on the horizon.

A shooting star streaked across the sky, and I made a wish. The one wish I knew was impossible now. But someday, maybe the rules could be changed, and I could be with Sarah for real, without putting her life in danger.

I KEPT STARING AT the clock, anxiously awaiting quitting time. I had packed my duffel this morning with all the clean clothing and had it behind my bedroom door, ready to collect and tie down to the back of my motorcycle. At least snow season hadn't started in earnest, so driving to school wouldn't be a game of slip and slide.

I collected the tip from my last table, cleared the dishes, and cleaned the table, getting it ready for the next patron. That was the end of my working career at Joe's Grill. It had served me well through high school. I took one last look around and then headed in back to clock out. My last paycheck would be direct deposited like all the others, and I'd be back in the money again— at least for a little while.

My father was wealthy, but I'd always worked for my keep. Not because he made me, but because I did not want to be indebted to the bastard. Not after the way he had treated me since the rest of our family died. I'm not sure whether he blamed me for their deaths because I was over at Johnson's house, or if he wished it had been me instead of Mom, Carl, and Casey, but after their deaths, he acted as though he were the only one in mourning. The wedge between us prior to that night became an unfixable chasm.

I sighed and pushed the card into the ancient time recorder, waited for the click and pulled it out, putting it back in the slot on the wall. I turned, intending to head to Maddy's office, but she and the gang had gathered behind me. I had been too far into my own thoughts to hear them.

"We wanted to give you a little going away gift." Maddy shoved a box into my hand with a beaming smile.

Heat filled my cheeks. I did not expect this from the staff. I ripped the funky paper off the square box and peeled open the lid. Inside was a mug wrapped in fabric. I pulled both out and laughed at the "You're Dead to Us" mug and one of the Joe's Grill T-shirts.

"Thanks," I said, and Maddy pulled me in for an awkward hug.

"Stay safe out there," she whispered in my ear. She lost her husband to an agency sting gone wrong, so she knew more about what I was walking into than I did, and I knew a fair amount.

"I will," I whispered. "Thanks for giving me this job."

"My pleasure." She gave me a squeeze and then released me, wiping at her eyes.

I gave everyone a nod and then hightailed it out of there before this lump in my throat turned into an embarrassing show of emotion. When I pulled into the driveway on my motorcycle, my father stood in the doorway with his arms crossed like an evil sentry. His gaze penetrated through me. I turned off the motorcycle and took off my helmet, leveling the same impassive gaze that my father regarded me with.

I swung my leg over the seat and hung my helmet on the handlebar. There was a bite to the air, and it smelled like snow was coming, which made the itch to get going settle into my bones.

But the way my father was blocking the doorway, I had a bad feeling that this wasn't going to be as easy an exit as I had hoped. I did not want a showdown. I didn't want this to come to blows.

"I don't want to fight," I said as I approached. "I just want to get my things and go." I slowed when I got close enough to be within arm's reach. He hadn't budged.

"Where do you think you're going?" His voice held a feral warning.

"Does it matter?"

He pressed his lips together and his nostrils flared. "Yes. I do not want you to put yourself in a position that will screw up your future."

I took a deep breath. "I can handle myself with Sarah."

His eyes narrowed. "I saw the way you defended her."

"I would have defended anyone in the same circumstances. It wouldn't matter who it was happening to. Seeing that vile shit turned my stomach, and I would have reacted the same damn way."

"You would have torn them to pieces?"

I opened my mouth to answer but nothing came out at first. "I would have stopped them by any means necessary." That I was sure of. I would have killed them for their transgression. It was my knee-jerk reaction in the presence of evil.

The muscles in my father's arms flexed, making his shirt bulge. "I saw what you did. That was irrational anger. You lost control."

I bit the edge of my lower lip. I had lost control. They were trying to violate my partner. "Yes. I did lose control. But that's because I was witnessing true evil. And that is my response to that shit." Admitting it to him stung. "Your worries about me fucking up with Sarah are unwarranted. Those consequences are not something I'm willing to gamble with."

"And what if she loses control with you?"

"Stop. Neither of us is going to cross the line. But if I stay here, I'm likely to throw a punch at you. And as much as that would feel good with the shit you've pulled on me, it isn't good for the pack." I met his gaze. "And me fucking around with Sarah not only puts her at risk, but it puts the pack at risk. I won't do that. So, please get out of my way so I can get my stuff and get the hell out of here before I lose my temper."

His face reddened and his glare sharpened.

It looked like getting out of here unscathed had just become a futile effort.

17

“IF YOU EVER HOPE to lead this pack, you'd do well to remember your impact on them. You must think of their needs above your own,” my father lectured from the stoop.

“What the hell are you talking about?”

“Leaving someone short-staffed, for instance.” He pursed his lips as he looked down his nose at me.

“Maddy said it wasn't a problem.” She had rearranged things to accommodate my request, but she didn't indicate that my leaving would provide a hardship to her the way my father insinuated.

"She wouldn't tell you otherwise. But you put your needs over the pack's needs." He reached inside the door and then tossed my duffel bag to me with more force than necessary.

"I would have had to give notice before the end of the break anyway," I argued. But guilt bit at the edges of my skin, making me fidget.

His eyebrow cocked, challenging me to say it wasn't a problem.

I knew better than to take the bait, even though he had gotten under my skin. I'd give the restaurant a call when I arrived at school just to make sure she didn't need me for the rest of the break. If she did, I'd find other sleeping arrangements.

I turned on my heel and headed to my bike, securing the duffel bag before I grabbed my helmet. "Let Johnson know I won't need a ride back to school."

"That's your responsibility," my father barked. Irritation laced every syllable.

"Fine," I muttered as I put on my helmet, and then situated myself on the bike so I'd be comfortable for the more than two-hour ride. With a kick of the starter, my hog rumbled to life. Without another look, I turned around and headed away from the house and the nightmare that was my father.

Halfway to the academy, the sky decided to dump an angry snow squall that matched my mood. My back tire slipped, and I caught myself, slowing the bike down to a reasonable speed for the conditions and not the breakneck speed I had been going. I didn't need to end up as roadkill.

The rest of the ride was very much a white-knuckle trip. The snow followed me as if I had my own dark cloud overhead. Truthfully, winter roads were not the best for a motorcycle, but I needed to get away from home, so I took the risk.

By the time I reached the academy, my muscles ached from the stress.

I unhooked the duffel bag, praying my clothes weren't soaked through, but with the heavier weight of the bag, they probably were. I didn't know whether I had enough surfaces in the room to hang my clothes to dry or not. It gave me another reason to be angry with my father. If he wasn't such a dick, I wouldn't have had to drive my motorcycle in a snowstorm.

With a sigh, I pulled my motorcycle cover out of the storage space under the seat and stowed my helmet in its place before I covered the bike, securing it with straps that went under the body of the machine so it wouldn't blow off in a windstorm.

I tucked the front tire in the bike rack that would be enough of a stabilizer to keep my motorcycle upright for the duration of the winter and then hiked up the hill from the student parking lot. I filtered through my keys until I found the one for the outer doors of the academy. Underneath the front door awning, I shook off the snow that had accumulated on my shoulders and in my hair just from the walk up the hill before I stepped in the building. I went straight to my room and peeled out of my soaked jeans and leather riding coat.

And then I checked out my duffel bag. Half the clothes were damp, and the other half soaked enough to be able to wring out water. At least they were clean. But it would take a day to dry all this shit. I took the time to hang things on everything I could find. When I finished, my room looked like a dry cleaner's back room.

I still had a pair of sweats and a couple T-shirts in my bureau, and I pulled them on before I fished out my phone from the inside pocket of my coat.

What are you up to? I texted Sarah.

Just hanging in the library. How'd work go?

I tucked the phone into my pocket and left my room, jogging barefoot down the hallway, and snuck into the library. She had her back to me, and I padded across the floor soundlessly. She jumped when I slid into the chair next to her.

"Work went fine." I grinned at her. "But I couldn't deal with the home situation, so I'm back for the rest of break."

She blinked at me. "How the hell did you get permission to stay? I had to jump through hoops to get them to let me hang here for winter break."

I glanced around and shrugged. No one else was in the library. "How many of you are here?"

"Just a couple of us." Her cheeks reddened. "And I couldn't tell you their names because they aren't in our classes." She leaned back in the seat and sighed as she pointed at me. "You are going to get in a shit ton of trouble."

"I'm a legacy and apparently the alpha here." I gave her my winning smile, as if that made all the difference in the world. But I would have to talk with someone about staying, and I hoped my actions wouldn't backfire on me.

"Well, then you'll be my guinea pig for the rest of the break." She beamed as if there were great rewards awaiting me.

"Doing what?" I shifted in the seat at the glint in her eye. My wolf fought for dominance but I kept him leashed and in control.

"You will be my taste tester with whatever concoction I put together in the kitchen." She waved at me as she spoke, as if I were royalty and going to be treated like it. It was damn cute.

I smirked at the grin playing on her lips. "So, I'll be eating a lot of charcoal?"

She swatted my arm with a laugh. "No. I only burned the first batch. I haven't made charcoal bricks since." Her chin jutted out with pride.

"Well, then I think I can do that, especially if you've already mastered brownies. There's nothing better than a warm brownie with a glass of cold milk."

"Actually, brownies in a bowl of milk is better." She closed the book she was reading and yawned. "You want some?" She didn't wait for an answer. She just grabbed my hand and pulled me out of the seat, dragging me along behind her.

Let's just say, I ate like a king over the rest of the winter break.

18

THE NEW SEMESTER SLID in with a blizzard, the likes of which hadn't been seen since the seventies, bringing with it subzero temperatures and intermittent power outages. On the third night without power, the staff brought all the students down to the cafeteria, where they lit the huge hearth for the first time in several years. Smoke belched out of the fireplace until the oversized chimney was hot enough to vanquish the cold air and allow the smoke to rise up the frigid shaft.

Even with all of us in the cafeteria, a roaring fire, and over a hundred wolves in all, we weren't able to get the room temperature beyond the mid-fifties. Sarah was huddled close enough to touch, and she shivered hard enough for her teeth to chatter in a constant click.

"Why don't you go sit near the fire for a little while?" I nodded toward several witches hogging the warmth. Most of whom she knew well enough to intrude upon.

"I'm fine." She stuttered her words between teeth clacking.

I nodded for Johnson to move to her other side. "You are going to get sick if you don't get warm."

She opened her mouth to argue, but I covered it with my hand.

I did not want to hear any of her arguments. "You'll owe me a decent pair of jeans." I pulled my hand away, shifting into my wolf. I glanced at Johnson, and he did the same. I curled up with my back against her side and Johnson shifted and leaned against her opposite side, sandwiching her with our warmth.

Other wolves in the room followed suit, huddling up against the nearest witch to give them some of our inherent warmth without making it inappropriate.

Sarah's chills subsided, and she stretched out between us, still bundled in her blankets. But she threw the edges over us. "Thank you."

I turned my head to look at her. I had to harness every emotion and every urge to claim her in that moment. Especially when her fingers slid over my brow of black fur and then gently scratched my ear. I closed my eyes and sighed before I stretched out on my side, with her weight against me.

By morning, the power was back, the fireplace held only embers, and we were sent back to our rooms so the staff could make breakfast. But it was the best night I've ever had. Sarah had kept her hand on my neck while she slept, and just the feeling of her that near me was more than enough to bring on that bitter taste of loss and regret as I padded my way back to my room with Johnson in tow.

He whined at me as we got closer to the room, but I didn't pay any attention to him. I was too lost in that dark space of knowing I would never get what I truly wanted in this life.

I shifted and opened our dorm room. Chilly air drifted over my naked form, and I held the door open for Johnson. He didn't shift until we were inside the room, where he could at least pull something on as quick as possible in the still frigid air.

After we both dressed, Johnson asked, "Are you okay?"

I huffed. "I will be." Knowing last night was the closest I'd ever get to sleeping with my soul mate stung like a beast.

"All I know is I haven't felt that kind of loss from you since your mother died."

I glanced at him. "You felt my mood?" It was common for the pack to feel their alpha's emotions if they were strong enough, but I wasn't the official alpha, yet.

He nodded. "Quite a few of us did."

Shit. That wasn't good. I didn't even have a viable excuse for it, either. And no one but Johnson and my father knew I had feelings for my partner. I not only had to muzzle my wolf, but I also needed to imprison my emotions from this point forward.

I threw myself facedown on the bed, mentally scolding myself for letting my emotions bleed through to the other wolves in the pack. "Just tell them I got blindsided with my mom and brother and sister's death again. Make up some shit about power outages and my mom cuddling with us to keep us warm."

I glanced over at him, and he actually looked impressed.

"That would be a viable story, but they've been dead a long time."

"It's all I got."

"I could add that all of us huddling together made you remember the good times before and then add your piece." Johnson raised an eyebrow like that was more believable.

I nodded. "Thanks." I closed my eyes. I hadn't gotten much rest last night with her body against mine.

"You coming to get something to eat?"

"I'm not really hungry. I'm going to catch a nap before classes start." I needed the time to also get my emotions in check before facing everyone.

"I'll come grab you after I eat."

I gave him a thumbs-up and the lull of sleep claimed me.

19

THE SEMESTER FLEW BY, and our last exam was one that took place in the gymnasium. With the class lined up, they had the first group step into the middle of the room, where thick cushy mats covered the floor. That first set of trainees had no warning before the line of agency officers raised their guns and shot.

The guns let out a *phew*, more like an air gun than bullets, but it still set off my alpha protective instinct. I went to take a step forward, but Sarah grabbed my forearm, defusing me enough to focus on the first line of students.

It wasn't bullets that hit the trainees. It actually looked like a dart. My brain stalled for a moment, trying to connect a memory to my current circumstance.

Tranquilizer. The thought barreled through my mind before the first witch fell unconscious. My father shot a rogue wolf once with one of those things. That rogue fell hard. And the wolves in the midst fell a few seconds after the witches. Now the oversized mats made a whole lot of sense.

The echo of dozens of students falling onto them still rang in the gym.

"Since you have the benefit of a warning, unlike these poor souls..." an instructor who none of us had ever seen in any of our training sessions said. He was short, at something like five six. If Sarah stood next to him, she would tower over him as though he were a dwarf. "Understand how you react when you wake from the tranquilizer will impact your ultimate station in the agency." He smiled, and it reminded me more of a weasel than a man.

I glanced at Sarah, but she was still staring at the others now being dragged off to the side of the gym and deposited on less forgiving mats. Buckets were placed by each person's head, as if they expected everyone who was tranquilized to vomit on waking.

My mouth turned into a bed of aluminum, and I tried to swallow it down. The idea of being that vulnerable bothered me, especially considering I was hiding a golly-whopper of a secret. And I had no idea what was in the tranquilizer.

We were next in line. When they waved us forward, I said, "Is this really necessary?" I had only made it a step or two at most when I felt the sting in my chest and looked down at the dart embedded in my skin.

Sarah faltered next to me, and I tried to catch her, but my muscles decided to stage a mutiny. I went down but didn't even feel the hit of the floor.

"HOLY FUCKING HELL," I whispered as knife shards pierced my brain. Even the light filtering in through my closed eyelids was painful. My stomach did a slow roll, and I clamped my mouth closed, slowly sucking air through my nose, willing myself not to hurl. The sounds of others doing just that filtered in.

I was glad I chose to get a few more minutes of sleep instead of food this morning, but between the headache, the sounds of retching, and the stench, I wasn't sure I'd be able to keep whatever acid was churning in my belly where it was.

Sarah.

The thought broke through the momentary paralysis, and I cracked my eyes open. I slowly moved my head to look around. Sarah was still unconscious next to me, but a few of the wolves in our line had already woken up. The first group all seemed to have their heads stuck in buckets.

The instructor was speaking, but I tuned him out, concentrating on the slow cadence of my breath. It seemed to be the only thing that allowed me not to throw up. And I kept at it until I heard her ungodly moan.

I cracked an eye, and she shot up so fast for the bucket, I thought she was possessed. Her entire body contracted with the heave, and I pulled myself up, gathered her hair and held it in a loose ponytail at her back. I rested my forehead on my hand, with her hair tickling my nose. Despite her horrific sounds, her hair still had that vague citrus scent that steadied my stomach.

After a while, she stopped heaving. "How are you not sick?" she whispered.

"I didn't eat this morning." Exams had drained the hell out of me and my choice to get some extra shut-eye seemed like a gift of fate. I would have been over a bucket, too, had I eaten breakfast. I let go of her hair and gave her some breathing room.

She slowly turned toward me as if moving might trigger her stomach again. The whites of her eyes carried a relief map of red veins as if she came close to blowing a vessel. Her face still held the paleness that everyone else in the room carried. "Thanks for holding my hair."

"I'm sure you'd do the same for me if I needed it."

"Yeah. No. I'd be out of here in a millisecond because if I did what you just did, I'd end up heaving all over you." She put her hand over her mouth and nose. "All this throwing up around us..." She didn't finish her sentence, and her throat bobbed as she held back another torrent.

I handed her my empty bucket and took hers to the men's room, flushing the contents down the toilet, and then I rinsed out the bucket. Before I went back into the gym, I threw cold water on my face and the back of my neck, hoping to make this headache go away. But it did nothing to ease it.

I made my way back into the gym as what looked like the last group went down with tranquilizers, which made me wonder how long we were actually out. Sarah leaned against the wall with a small can of ginger ale that the instructor was handing out to everyone.

"When you can get up, please head into the auditorium," the instructors requested.

I grabbed a soda as I passed the weasel-like man and helped Sarah to her feet.

"You must have a stomach made of iron," she muttered, taking small sips as she walked.

"It was just a stroke of luck." I led her into the auditorium and grabbed one of the seats near the back. Settling in, I cracked open the soda and took a small sip, closing my eyes as the cool fizzle slid down my throat. For a moment, I didn't know whether my stomach would accept it. After a few slow breaths, my belly growled at the lack of contents, and hunger set in. I drained the small can and crushed it in my hand, hoping it would ease the pangs now gripping my belly.

Sarah glanced sideways at me. "Even the sound of the can crunching hurts my head."

"Sorry." I tossed the crumpled metal into the garbage by the door. The aluminum hitting the metal made a loud clang and Sarah winced.

"Did you even get tranquilized?"

Her exasperation nearly made me smile.

"Yes. And I'm not exactly feeling chipper." I leaned my head back and closed my eyes. "It should fade in a couple hours," I added.

"That weaselly guy told me the same before he handed me the soda." The sound of sipping followed before she continued. "He also said it was a half dose. I can't imagine what a full dose would do."

"Probably a lot of the same, just knocked out for longer." I kept my eyes closed even though the assembly room was dark enough to not shoot stinging shards of light into my irises like a thousand tiny needles.

"True." She sighed and shifted in the seat.

I opened the eye closest to her as she scrunched down far enough to lean her head against the back edge of the chair. She had the right idea, but my height didn't allow me to slouch as much as she could. I rolled my neck and crossed my arms, watching as the assembly room filled with pale students sporting the same tranquilizer hangover.

The lights slowly came up and the entire crowd groaned in response, me included.

"My name is Harrison Littleton. I am a senior trainer from the head office in New York City," the weaselly-looking man said from the stage as if he were better than all of us here in the room. He couldn't have been much more than ten years older than we were, but between his superior attitude and the fact he didn't have any scent of magic or wolf on him, that only meant one thing.

"I think he's just human," I whispered to Sarah. I knew there were at least a handful of high-ranking humans on the board of the Monster Defense Agency, because my father always grumbled about them being totally useless.

"How can you tell?"

I glanced at her. Had she not retained anything we learned this last semester? When she looked at me with her bleary brown eyes, I pointed at my nose.

"Oh, yeah," she whispered, and her cheeks reddened. "Sorry. It's hard to think with this headache." She rubbed her temples, still looking a little peaked.

I thought about razzing her, but my headache had just gone from manageable with the dark room to splitting again with the lights. And I woke up before she did. So, I gave her a pass this time.

I glanced back at the stage and Harrison Littleton, who droned on about graduation. The only thing that caught my attention and had Sarah sitting up more was when he started talking about assignments and what would happen next.

By the time this graduation ceremony was finished, all the assignments would be cataloged and printed out and hung on the board outside the auditorium. We would know where we were going as soon as we walked out this door to pack up our things.

That perked a lot of us up. I glanced around and found Johnson staring back at me, as if he needed reassurance that I did indeed make it through the ordeal. I hadn't even looked for the rest of my pack in the gym. I was too concerned with Sarah and that weighed on me. I sent him a halfhearted nod. I needed to be better than that in the future. I scanned the audience and met several sickly looking gazes with the same nod of approval for making it through the academy.

At least, wherever I was going, the Allegany pack would follow—unless my father screwed me even further. After our last encounter, I wouldn't put it past him.

The man kept droning on and then he finally announced the academy's headmaster. Mr. Simmons stepped up to the podium and praised us for being one of the finest classes the academy had ever seen despite some challenging times earlier in the year. Our grades and physical stamina had far outpaced some of the more recent graduates and we were sure to become fine agents in the field.

"The reason we do graduation after the tranquilization test is to assess your ability to focus after. And for the top student in the class, the bar is even higher. You have the honor and privilege of stepping up on stage to say a few words to your fellow students." He smiled and scanned the audience back and forth, and then his gaze pulled back to me before he looked down at the paper before him. "This year's top student has become an exceptional leader. He's the best and brightest we've seen in these halls since his father graduated years ago."

"Fuck," I whispered, because I knew what was coming and I was not prepared for it.

"Mr. Robert Young Junior, will you please join me on stage."

Sarah snickered beside me as I climbed to my feet.

I looked down at her. "I should drag your ass up there with me."

"I wouldn't be caught dead on stage in front of all these people, Junior." She gave me that playful smile, needling me with the one part of my name I hated.

"And bring your spirited partner with you," Mr. Simmons added after looking at the notes handed to him. "Because her scores are just as impressive."

I grinned down at her. "Now you don't have a choice."

She paled as she looked at the stage and then me with pure panic.

I felt her terror in my bones and faltered for a moment. This fierce woman suffered from stage fright? She could kick ass in the gym in front of the entire class, but the idea of standing on stage made her even more sickly looking. I extended my hand, hoping I wouldn't have to do anything drastic to get her moving.

"Come on. I promise, you won't have to talk. You can even hide behind me if you need to," I said softly enough that very few around us heard me.

She tentatively took my hand and followed behind me like a scolded puppy. If I wasn't feeling every nuance of her fear, I would have found it amusing. I climbed up on stage and released her hand, smiling at Mr. Simmons, who waved me to the podium.

"Say a few words to your graduating class," he said.

I stepped up to the microphone and glanced out at the class. "It seems my partner here, while ferocious in the sparring ring, suffers from a bit of stage fright, so I'll speak for the both of us when I say it has been a pleasure and an honor to study beside each of you." I scanned the crowd again, zeroing in on all the Allegany pack members and their partners before moving my gaze over the rest of my classmates.

I glanced back at Sarah and then pulled my focus back to the group. "Being a leader, an alpha, means taking care of your pack. There are plenty of alphas here, and when you get to your destination, make sure you understand who your pack consists of. Here, everyone in this room was part of my pack. Out there, it could be infinitely larger, and you may not be the lead honcho, so show whoever is in that role the respect they deserve." I took a breath. "Remember your purpose. And remember to have a little fun as well."

A few members whooped and then winced, like they had momentarily forgotten they had tranq-hangover. I smiled.

I glanced back at Sarah and saw a hint of a smile appear.

The fact this was the last time I would see most of these people hit. I was going to truly miss this. "So, are you ready to get out there and kick some vampire ass?" I raised my arm.

This time, it seemed my call to celebrate was met with more enthusiasm. Many raised their arms and yelled, "Hell yeah!"

I stepped back and took Sarah's hand, raising it in the air with mine, and the audience started to clap. It was exhilarating.

I gave Mr. Simmons a smile and a partial bow before I stepped to leave the stage.

"Whoa there, you two," he said. "Don't you want to know your assignment?"

We both swung back toward the podium, and my muscles tightened with anticipation.

Mr. Simmons looked at the paper in his hand and grinned. "You two are headed to the Big Apple."

"Headquarters?" I asked. That's where the hot-bed of vampire activity happened on a daily basis and had for years. It was also one of the most dangerous assignments you could get in the agency.

"Yes. Headquarters."

I straightened my back, glanced at Sarah, and then gave a nod. "Sounds about right." I searched the crowd. As much as I wanted a countryside station, the thought of being able to tear through vampires at the rate that the agents at headquarters did made me shiver with anticipation. "I'm all for being in the capital of vampiric activity." I grinned. "And I am looking forward to slaying as many blood suckers as possible."

20

S O, NEW YORK CITY was not ideal, but at least it was where most vampires seemed to congregate on the East Coast. Johnson, Hannah, and a few others from the Allegany pack were assigned here with us, but it was by no means the bulk of my pack. The rest had gone home to the backwoods of New York and didn't have to deal with the light pollution or sound pollution that was driving me batty.

The living arrangements were no better than at the academy. The small efficiency apartments were no bigger than the dorm rooms had been and they packed everything in that space: kitchen, bedroom, and bathroom with no real living space. It was claustrophobic as hell. Especially considering we were living in the same building where we worked.

I needed my own space, but I had three years before the trust fund my mother left me activated. Then I would be able to buy almost anything I wanted. I kept my eye on the real estate sales and the different areas I wanted to live in. Brooklyn was by far the best option, and there were some upscale areas that I had my eye on. Sarah wasn't looking down near Brooklyn. She was looking up in the Harlem area, which was more affordable, and the homes were a bit smaller.

She had to wait until she turned eighteen to access her parents' estate, but her birthday was in December. She only had to get through the summer and fall before she was free of this place.

So, we dealt with communal living and learned the rituals we all needed to keep safe, like always having our weapons on us, both blades and guns, as well as wearing our anti-compulsion charms, so vampires couldn't compel us. That was the most dangerous part of dealing with a blood sucker. If you didn't have your charms on, you were dead.

I itched to get out there and slay some vampires, but we weren't cleared for field work yet. Instead, we sparred, studied, ate, and slept until Harrison Littleton thought we were ready. He was militant on the rules, to the point of reaching beyond a boss. He was more like a dictator, and I had to stanch my aggravated alpha wolf any time I dealt with the asshole.

Sarah and I sparred regularly. She was getting even faster now that she had other agents to spar with who did not hold back. Same with me, it was refreshing to be challenged, and stung when I got my ass kicked. At least that was getting rarer these days.

We were sparring when Sarah and I were called into Harrison's office.

He looked frazzled in a way we hadn't seen since we arrived. His hair stood out in spikes, as if he had been running his hands through it and his cheeks wore the blotchy redness of irritation. "I need you two to go to this address." He handed me a piece of paper. "It's a suspected vampire nest, so things might get hairy." He sucked in a breath of air through his nose. "Usually, for a thing like this, I'd send the entire force, but I have been instructed to send you two."

I raised an eyebrow at that. *Why would they choose to send two new recruits instead of seasoned agents?* "Why?"

"Because my more experienced agents are dealing with another, more pressing issue, and I cannot divert them to a suspected nest until they are finished with the job they are on. And of the newbies here, you two are the only ones who seem to be fit for the job. I'm not one to send agents to the slaughter, either, but those higher than me think you two will be fine."

Either that or the higher ups really want us dead. I shook that thought out of my head and focused on the assignment.

"What constitutes a nest?" Sarah asked, seemingly satisfied with Harrison's answer.

"More than half a dozen vampires living in a home."

Sarah put her hand out and a katana sword materialized in her palm. It was the perfect killing weapon to separate the vampire's head from their body, which, outside of dragging them into the sunshine, was the only way to kill a blood sucker for good. Although tearing their hearts out sounded fun, they weren't alive, so it would just leave a hole in their chest, which would heal by the next sunset.

She handed the sword to me with a smile and pulled another one for herself from the ether. Harrison's lips curled into a frown. He did not have high regard for witches. He thought they were as tainted as any of the others, including werewolves. But wolves were far superior in intelligence, speed, and strength enough so that he begrudgingly respected us.

"Just make sure you have your charm on," Harrison said. "And take a cab. Your motorcycle is too noisy. They'll hear you coming from miles away."

I pulled the chain from under my shirt, showing that I had it on. Sarah did the same, and then we changed into street clothes and were off on our first job. My heart pounded as I read the paper. "You might want to hang onto these until we get there." I gave Sarah the sword. "I doubt we'll get a cab holding these."

"You're probably right." The metal in her hands disappeared as if it never had been there. "But the minute we get out of the cab, I'm retrieving them."

"Fine by me." I raised my hand, hailing a cab. It took a couple of minutes before one pulled up to the curb. We piled in the back, and I rattled off the address. I pulled out my wallet and peeled out a twenty for the fare, shoving my wallet into the interior pocket of the worn leather coat that Sarah conjured for me at that first dinner at the academy. When we got out, I didn't want to be shuffling through my wallet. I wanted a clean drop-off, so we had more of an element of surprise.

Vampires would smell us coming, so the longer we lingered on the street, the more prepared for our attack they would be. Assuming they were even awake, considering it was near noon and the sun blazed down. At least it was cool enough to wear the jacket. Spring days in New York City could be a scorcher, but this one had been blessedly cool.

"Drop us off a few houses down, please," I added when we finally turned onto the road.

The driver looked in the rearview mirror with a nod. The minute he pulled over, I shoved the twenty through the slot, even though the fare was a hair less than ten bucks. I nodded for Sarah to go and slid out the passenger door after her. "Keep the change." I slammed the door and took a deep breath as the cab pulled away.

I glanced at the numbers and spotted the one we needed to check out. It was New York City. The doors were likely locked, and the house was in the middle of a bank of row houses. I just hoped the occupants of the homes on either side were at work because this was likely to be a hell of a ruckus.

The shades were all drawn in the unit we were hitting. The ones on either side weren't, so that was another indicator and one of the things we needed to target once we got inside. Sunlight was our friend, and the more shades we were able to open, the safer we would be.

I glanced at Sarah. "Can you conjure the door key?"

She put out her hand; her lips moved as she read off the address from the sheet of paper and a key appeared in her palm.

She really did have the coolest magic.

"Target the shades first," I said. "That way we at least have a safe place if the shit hits the fan."

"Good plan." She handed me the key and then put her palms up. A moment later, the swords appeared. She held onto mine, and we approached quickly. I slid the key into the hole and turned. The click of the lock disengaging made me smile, and we entered the house quickly. I traded the key for a sword and closed the door behind us, enveloping us in darkness.

Sarah reached out, grabbing my arm.

I could see in the dark. She couldn't. We moved toward the living area on the right, where I had seen the shades, but on this side, big panels of wood blocked the entire window, and they were nailed in place.

"Fuck." That's when the stench of death hit me. My heart thundered at the shuffling from the far side of the room. Vampires were uncurling from their positions on the floor and climbing to their feet. The man on the couch curled his lips back, baring teeth as his glare met mine.

There were more in the back rooms; I was sure of it just by the smell.

The only way Sarah would survive this was if she could see what she was swinging at. I had a second to scan the wall. Luck was with us, and I reached out and flipped the light switch right next to where we stood, bathing the room in light.

Now she could see them. Outside of being pale, vampires didn't look that different from humans or witches or werewolves in human form, except for the fangs and the red eyes. Oh, and another difference that rang through the room was the hideous hiss they made. It made me twitch. That hiss hit a pitch that hurt my wolf ears.

My guess was right; that hiss brought forth more from the back rooms. This was a nest all right, but there were more than a dozen vampires in this house. I backed up toward those wooden shutters with Sarah at my side and my grip on the sword tightened.

"Double fuck," Sarah whispered, but there wasn't the fear I expected.

I glanced at her and blinked at the crazy smile on her lips. Although her heart pounded as frantically as mine, it was as if the shot of adrenaline woke up the kick ass side of her. This was my battle queen, and fuck if I didn't want to claim her right now.

We focused on the group of vampires stalking toward us.

"Stay still," the leader who had risen from the couch said in a commanding tone that would have frozen us in place had we not had the charms on.

Sarah stepped far enough away from me so that her swing wouldn't harm me, and she positioned herself at the ready. "I don't think so, motherfuckers." She didn't wait for them to descend on us. I had a brief moment to witness her cunning and skill as she beheaded the lead vampire. Then I jumped into the fray.

Heads rolled, literally. But when Sarah cried out, my wolf took control at the sight of a vampire with their teeth in her arm. The same fury that had captured me in her dorm room rushed through my veins, and I leapt at the vampire accosting her, tearing his torso in two. It was enough to dislodge his teeth, but it also left a bloody gouge in her arm.

She didn't stop fighting, and I turned my sights on the rest of the nest, decapitating as many with my jaws as she was with her katana. One of them dodged my attack and launched at me, hitting my shoulder with teeth as sharp as mine.

I yelped and the whistle of a blade slicing through air followed. Although the teeth were still embedded in my skin, the rest of the body fell to the floor. I met Sarah's gaze with a nod before we took down the remaining vampires.

When there weren't any more attacking, we glanced around at the carnage. Sarah was covered with blood and her open wound still seeped. Thankfully, you couldn't be turned just from vampire blood alone; otherwise we would both be screwed. I limped over to one of the windows and took the bottom edge of the board between my teeth. I yanked and nails creaked. I yanked again and the bottom portion ripped from the wall.

Sarah moved to the corner away from where I was trying to get the window covering off. Anywhere else in the room would be dangerous because when this mother gave way, wood would fly. I kept pulling.

She dialed a number on her phone. "It's clear, but we could use a little medical attention." She glanced at her arm and then at me, where the vamp head was still attached. "We both were bitten. Me on the arm and Robby has a decapitated head still clamped on his shoulder."

The wood creaked some more and then all of a sudden it gave, ripping drywall with the force and spraying white dust into the room. I tossed the wood toward the far corner where there were no bodies and then tore the shade right off with another yank of my teeth. It fluttered to the ground, and the sun bathed me with warmth. The head still attached to my shoulder burst to ashes, leaving only a bloody welt. Any of the bodies in the path of the sunlight did the same, leaving a plume of ash in the air.

"His vamp is now ash, but there still are puncture wounds," she said as I headed her way. "He's in wolf form for now as well."

I limped over to Sarah and licked her wound, cleaning it as best I could before I curled up next to her, putting my head on her leg. Now that the adrenaline had faded to nothing, the reality of what happened hit hard enough to make my wolf form shake. Fear laced my mouth at what could have happened today, and I did not want to shift back to human form so she could see this side of me.

It would be too transparent. Too readable. She would know in an instant that I was in love with her. The slow stroke of her hand on my head and her soft coos of "shhh" were nearly more than my wolf could take.

The minute the cavalry arrived, I shifted back to human form, so I could relay the details of the encounter along with Sarah. And my partner, the goddess that she was, clothed me with a wave of her hand. But the jacket she had given me was in shreds on the floor. I went to it and fished out my wallet, sliding it into my back pocket. I loved this damn coat.

I caught her staring at me, and I shrugged, holding up the coat.

"I'll conjure you another one when we get back," she said as a medic tended to her arm.

"Thanks." I glanced at what I could see of my wound. It still oozed where the vampire had latched on. Even though I had been in wolf form, the wounds didn't heal as fast as they normally would. Something in the vampire's saliva slowed down my healing capabilities.

When the medic finished with Sarah, he took a look at my punctures and put a bandage over it before he loaded us into the agency ambulance.

The adrenaline had fled and all that was left was an exhaustion pummeling my muscles. Sarah looked about the same as I felt. With our first mission came our first injuries. But I also got to see Sarah in action, and she was fierce and strong and relentless.

I wondered how many more times I would get to witness her being such a badass and still be able to control my wolf.

Someday my wolf would win, and he would damn us both.

21

FIFTEEN YEARS LATER...

I stepped into the conference room for our daily morning brief and scanned the room for the crop of red hair. But she was absent. I hadn't run into her in the pit either, and my gut clenched.

Over the past year, the connection I had with Sarah seemed wonky. She seemed more closed off, as if she were hiding something, but under that secrecy, she seemed to be truly happy, as though she had met someone. Which was enough to make my wolf rant all the louder. And then, a few weeks ago, it changed into something like grief. I even saw it in her eyes each day, but she still didn't open up to me. Her sudden change unhinged me, and now her being late just scrambled my insides.

Sarah was never late. Me, on the other hand—I wasn't as punctual to a fault as she was. Maybe she was in the restroom. But the growing alarm inside didn't pipe down at that viable excuse.

I took my normal seat and waited, fidgeting in my chair as the seconds ticked by. Harrison walked in and closed the door, sauntering to the front of the room to start the meeting.

The chair remained empty next to me and that sense in the pit of my stomach that something was wrong grew to a nearly unmanageable level. *Where are you?* I texted her.

Overslept. Not feeling very good. Cover for me?

I stared at the reply. If it was anyone else, I might have taken it at face value, but Sarah was never sick. Even if she had a bender the night before, she was in here, looking green and gross. My abdomen knotted.

The moment the meeting ended, I tried to make a quick exit, but Harrison caught me before I could get away.

"Where's Stone?" He nodded toward the now-empty briefing room.

The first excuse that popped into my head, tumbled from my lips. "She said she thinks she may have had some bad food last night. I'm going to head over and check on her. I'm not sure whether to bring coffee or soup." I gave the boss a dubious smile, praying it wouldn't cause too many questions.

"Coffee might be your best bet. And tell her she needs to get her ass into the office as soon as possible. You two need to chase down the last lead we have on the dumpster vampire before the trail disappears. There hasn't been a body in three weeks. Either he has taken a vacation or there's going to be a bloodbath in New York City."

I nodded and headed out to the car, texting as I walked. *Coming over with coffee.*

In the shower, give me a few minutes.

Well, at least she was out of bed. That familiar tingle ran up my spine, and my wolf struggled against the binds I've kept him in for the last fifteen years. Against all odds, I've kept him in line. Although it has made both of us more volatile on the hunt. When I let him loose to kill, he's vicious to a fault.

I stopped at the nearest coffee shop and grabbed her favorite coffee and one for myself, and then headed to her house. That uneasy feeling had bloomed, making my wolf restless.

Pulling into her small driveway did nothing to ease my nerves. The moment she swung the door open, my wolf nearly burst forth at the smell of death radiating from inside. I held onto the coffee cups in my hands, praying that it was something else. But one more sniff told me otherwise.

What the fuck?

"Sarah?" I cocked my head, searching her face.

"It's been a tough morning." She sighed and swung the door wide, waving me inside.

Fuck. Fuck. Fuck. This cannot be happening!

Every muscle burned. My mouth went dry, and I cautiously stepped over the threshold. My knuckles turned white with the strain of not crushing the cups in my hands. I offered her one and was thankful my hand didn't shake.

She reeked like a vampire, but there was an alluring scent competing with the dead stench surrounding her. When she took a sip of coffee, my brain stalled. Vampires didn't drink anything but blood.

I glanced around the entry, looking for another explanation. Nothing presented itself, so I glanced back at her. "You're... You smell different." I closed the door behind me.

"I had this house locked up tight and warded." She turned and headed into the kitchen as her stomach rumbled.

She didn't turn back to look at me. A panic that I couldn't contain slid through me like a tornado, and my wolf whispered to mark her. That was the only logical thing that would keep her safe. I ignored his incessant whining. When she didn't continue, I asked, "And?"

She spun back to face me with eyes that pleaded for me to understand, but she didn't speak. My heart jumped in my chest, and I licked my lips, trying to put the muzzle back on my wolf's rantings.

"And?" I asked with more force. The cup in my grip crushed, spraying coffee everywhere. The sting of hot liquid on my skin gave me a much-needed slap of sanity. But it was short-lived.

Sarah pulled a vial full of coagulated blood out of her pocket and handed it to me. "This was all over my bedroom floor and walls."

I shook the hot coffee from my hand and snatched the vial from her. I didn't want to know what was inside. I rolled it between my fingers, as though I could change the contents just by moving the thick liquid this way and that. "You know I'm obligated to report this," I said with the regret of a thousand missed opportunities in my voice.

"I don't want to be locked up like Manuel." She shifted her stance into ready form, as if she prepared for a fight.

I almost laughed at her. I wasn't going to fight her. We hadn't talked about what happened to Manuel. I already knew her stance, but I couldn't condone having him out on the streets. But this was Sarah. *My Sarah.*

I couldn't fathom locking her up. Hell, I knew I'd never report this, despite what I said. I crossed and towered over her, invading her personal space. Being this close to her set that inferno that had been burning for fifteen years to the unmanageable level. She was already doomed by whatever had happened.

"Do you really think I'd lock you up?" I studied her face and willed my hands not to reach out to cup her cheeks and take her mouth with mine. Logically, I had nothing to lose anymore. But my heart needed convincing. I had been protecting her from my wolf for so long that it was a natural reaction. If I let my wolf have his way, there was no saving either of us.

Her brow creased and her gaze narrowed up at me. "What?"

"I'd tear your throat out before I'd let you rot in a cell for the rest of eternity." But that wasn't going to happen, either. Not with my wolf demanding what he wanted all along.

She swallowed hard and dropped her gaze to my chest. Her fear blanketed me.

I lost the battle and reached out, cupping her chin and forcing her to look at me. "You aren't built for captivity."

I hated that I couldn't speak freely with her. But my point still held. Neither one of us were built to be caged for the rest of our lives.

I got hold of myself and let go, moving back to give her space and clear my head.

"Asshole," she muttered and rubbed her chin.

That was uncalled for, and I realized what nonsense had tumbled out of my mouth. I guess I would have reacted the same way if I stood in her shoes and my partner just told me they'd rather kill me than lock me away for life.

"You would do the same for me," I said, trying to soften the harshness of my original statement. I'm sure she could follow through with a threat like that, too. Sarah was a force. She had always been one. But no matter the threat, I would never harm her or lock her up. Ever.

My heart clenched in my chest. I was doomed.

I glanced at the blood in the tiny container and pressed my lips together, saying a prayer to the gods above that this wasn't hers. I unscrewed the lid and took a sniff. That sweet smell of lemons and caramel coffee drifted out of the vial, and I closed my eyes. "It's your blood."

Two conflicting emotions hit like a Category 5 hurricane making landfall: devastation because Sarah was *other*, and my wolf was doing a fucking jig like this was the best possible situation.

"Just run it through the database," she insisted.

It was enough to send a rash of uncomfortable heat over my skin. Alarm settled into my cells, and I glanced at the blood and then shook my head slowly. "If I do that, it will raise questions."

"But aren't you obligated..."

I put my splayed hand out, silencing her. "If I run this through the database, yes, I'm obligated. So, I am not going to run it through just to confirm what I can already smell. And what any wolf at headquarters will smell the moment you walk in. You are...*other*." I snarled out the last part, fighting my base nature.

Sarah collapsed into the chair at the kitchen table.

"What happened?" I asked but did not venture any closer. I needed distance to think, and my mind had already started thinking of ways for her not to be tracked down like the rest of the vampires we hunted. Those always ended with a dead body, and I couldn't allow that to happen to her.

"I have no clue." She shrugged and pushed away the coffee with a scowl. "I went to sleep and then woke up with my room painted with blood, but there wasn't a drop on the sheets. It only covered the walls and the floor, like my bed itself had been covered by some magic spell to keep it pristine." She lifted her chin and held out her wrists so I could see the unblemished skin. "There isn't a goddamned mark on me, so how could I have bled out like that, and be sitting here talking to you this morning like nothing happened?"

I stepped closer and started to shake with the need welling up inside me. "You need to quit," I said as my gaze darted all around the room at everything but her. It was a stupid statement. I knew there was no quitting. That carried the same death sentence as relationships. But my mouth kept betraying me in the onset of panic. "Tell them you found something less stressful."

She burst out laughing at this whole ludicrous situation. "Quitting is a death sentence. You know that as well as I do. Besides, they won't buy it."

She was right. They knew she was as much of an adrenaline junkie as I was. *Fuck.* Here goes nothing. "Then tell them you need to quit because you want a relationship with me."

Her laughter exploded into that of hysterics, and my panic morphed into a hot anger. "You don't think they'd buy that?"

"Would you?" she sputtered through her laughter.

Irrational irritation gripped me, and I spiked the glass vial onto the kitchen floor. It shattered, bathing the room in the scent of her blood, and my wolf took control. I crossed the distance and pulled her out of the seat, slammed her into the closest wall, and battled with my wolf as she stared directly into my eyes.

"What the—" she started.

My wolf won.

I crushed her lips with mine in a forbidden kiss. Her mouth opened, and I wasn't sure whether it was in surprise or in response to my kissing her, but I took full advantage of it, teasing her tongue with mine.

In that moment, I knew I lost the battle. My wolf was now in control, and I'd never get it back. Not now that I'd tasted her. Other or not, my wolf wanted her.

Then her knee connected with my balls and that moment died with a flare of pain. I dropped her and started to fall to my knees when she pushed me hard enough to fall back on my ass.

"Don't you ever fucking manhandle me," she yelled. "We may be partners, but that is where we have always drawn the line."

Flames leapt from her hair, her hands—even her face—and my eyes widened. *She's on fire!* I glanced at the window as I moved back, still holding my aching balls, but the light was all wrong.

Sarah ran her hand through her hair as if she had no clue, and then she looked toward the reflection in the microwave door. Her eyes ballooned wide and then she raised her hands, looking at the same red flames that I was.

All of the sudden, the flames went out and she was my Sarah again. Except, this was something insane. No vampire we knew of had ever broken out in flame like she just had. Unless they were dragged out into the sunshine, and that was usually accompanied by screams before they turned to ash.

"Sarah?"

She shook her head at the question in my voice. She was just as thrown by all this as I was.

What the hell had attacked her last night?

I got my bearings and crawled to the table, pulling myself up into the chair.

"Do you need some ice?" Sarah asked, but her voice still shook.

"I'll live. But a coffee would be nice, since mine is all over your entry." I hooked my thumb over my shoulder.

She nodded and it was as if she were glad to be doing something normal after that display of whatever the fuck that was. I don't blame her; the sounds of the coffee machine calmed me down enough to think past her lips on mine.

She put a cup in front of me and took the seat opposite me, putting the table between us, as if that solid barrier could keep us from breaking the rules again.

"Do I feel cold to you?" she asked out of the blue and then slid her hand across the table.

I hesitated. Touching her would reignite that inferno, and it was all consuming. But the plea in her eyes had me reaching out to cover her hand. Her warmth seeped into my palm, and I kept my hand in place longer than I should have.

"No. You feel normal."

She rolled her eyes at me and then looked at her wrist. "I'm half tempted to cut myself to see if I bleed."

"Don't," I said. "I'm barely containing my wolf as it is." I waved toward the wall where I had kissed her, hoping she would understand.

"What's that supposed to mean?" She leaned back in her chair and crossed her arms.

Ah, fuck. Another goddamned rabbit hole that I don't need to jump into. I pressed my lips together and shook my head.

"Well?" She stared at me waiting for an explanation that I did not want to get into.

"Sarah—"

She cut me off. "Stop with that tone. I'm not fragile, so don't you dare treat me that way." She pointed at me like one of our instructors at the academy. "Besides, you're the one who brought up your wolf, so just speak your mind like we've always done. *This* shouldn't change that."

I couldn't help the snicker. She really didn't know how I felt about her. "Well, my wolf isn't sure whether to tear you to pieces or..." I trailed off with a shrug, although a dimple made a quick appearance.

"Or what?" She leaned forward, catching my gaze.

"My wolf can't seem to decide between tearing you apart or fucking you. If you spill more of your blood, I'm not sure I can contain him." I met her gaze, a little exasperated for having to spell it out.

"You want to...fuck me?" Her voice cracked, and she leaned back in the chair.

"My wolf." I swallowed and stared at the table. Damn it. She had enough schooling on werewolves to know that my wolf's desires were just a magnification of what was already in my heart.

"And this sudden urge was triggered by my change?"

I just lifted a single shoulder and glanced out the window. I was damning both of us by admitting this to her, but I couldn't lie to her. Not when she asked such a direct question.

"Why wait to tell me this until now?" she asked quietly. The question was filled with something more.

I slowly forced my gaze to meet hers, baring every emotion I had locked inside for all these years. She drew in a breath and her eyes widened as if she finally saw the truth. "We are *supposed* to be partners. They kill witches who cross the line. You *know* that."

She opened her mouth to speak, and her phone rang. She put it to her ear without breaking eye contact with me. "Sarah Stone."

Her face paled at whatever the caller said. Then her hands burst into flame again and she dropped the phone onto the table.

I moved to her side. "Who was that?"

"I, uh. I don't know." She wrapped her arms around herself and shivered. Her hand splayed across her throat in almost a protective reflex.

Seeing her so disturbed broke another piece of that wall surrounding my wolf, and I crouched next to her, touching her arm. The connection shot a jolt of heat through me, and all I wanted to do was take her in my arms and claim her. "You don't know?"

"No. But I suppose we should hunt this bastard down."

Oh, fuck no. "You can't work. You can't go near anyone from the office. Not with how you smell."

"How do I smell?"

"You smell like death already claimed you. Like almost every damn vampire I've killed has. But it is mixed with something sweet and light and tangy that makes my wolf want to claim you right this moment to keep you safe and protected. It's strangely abhorrent and alluring at the same time." Words just tumbled out of me like a damn leaky faucet. I blinked, trying to gain some sense of control.

"Different than before?"

I smiled. "Before, you smelled like caramel coffee with a side of lemon cake."

She narrowed her eyes at me. "That's my daily coffee shop order."

"And it suited you. As sweet as that was to take in daily, this"—I waved at her—"along with the vibes you are transmitting, will set off every single supernatural alarm within blocks of wherever you go." I forced myself to stand, to get a little distance. "Stay here while I take a look around. I'm going to see if I can detect a trace of this bastard."

God, her bedroom smelled like blood and bleach, and I nearly gagged from it. Death was here, and I could almost see her struggle. The fact I could still smell her death over the bleach was a testament to how much had been drained from her body. And it was all over the place. Despite her scrubbing, I could see the traces left behind.

I growled and stopped at the entrance to her reading nook. The chair held the smell of death, and it was strong enough to tell me the vampire who attacked her had been in it for a while. But there was another scent overlaying it, the same way the bleach overlayed the blood, that made me remember a time early in our career when Heddie successfully did a masking spell on Hannah. It smelled like sandalwood and spice then. That's what the overlaying scent was. A fucking masking spell.

The window had the sigil on it, but it was open, making the warded barrier useless.

I went back to the kitchen, deep in concentration, and took my seat across from her. "Are you sure you set up all your wards properly?"

"Yes. Why?" She glanced at me.

"I smelled something with the same dark signature, but it seemed to be masked. Like whoever was here had traces of magic on his being. And he was here long enough for his smell to permeate your sitting chair by the window. And your window is open."

She blinked at me, as if she didn't comprehend what I was saying.

"Could you have left it open?"

"I swear, every window and door was closed and warded. Including that one. Besides, it is not warm enough for me to leave my window open at night." She crossed her arms. "I don't have a built-in heater like you do."

I stared into my empty cup with a nod. "I'll tell the boss you're dealing with food poisoning. You need to stay here until I can find out a little more."

"Bullshit. I need to find this asshole and slice off his head."

My gaze widened at her words, and I shook my head. I couldn't let her do that. If she killed her maker, she would die, too.

22

I WALKED INTO THE agency, chewing my lip while deep in thought. *How was I going to get her out of this?*

Harrison cut me off.

"Where's your partner?" he asked with his eyes narrowed in suspicious slits.

"She's got a pretty bad case of food poisoning. I tried to talk her into going to a hospital, but she didn't want to leave the bathroom."

"Are you sure that's it?" He seemed to growl the words.

"Dude, it's coming out both ends, so yes, I'm sure. It's either that or a wicked case of the stomach bug, but she doesn't have a fever." I glanced behind Harrison at the pit. "Didn't Karen have a bug recently?" I asked. Karen was his administrative assistant, and she was out for a few days with a stomach thing.

He muttered under his breath. "Yes. But Sarah's never been sick."

"Yeah, well, you can see for yourself, but if it's contagious, you'll probably get it just by standing outside the door." Harrison was a bit of a germaphobe, and I used that to my advantage. After Karen called in, he scrubbed down his office and her desk with enough bleach so it even stung the noses of the witches in the pit. It was unbearable for us wolves, and we fled the floor until the stench dissipated.

"What do you have for me today?" I asked, making him focus on something other than Sarah, and hoping for something light enough that I could do some research.

"I was going to ask Johnson to divert and gather resources for Manuel, but since you're not with your loudmouth partner, I think you'd be perfect to gather a stock of blood."

As much as I didn't want to do that, at least I'd have a legitimate reason to pilfer blood banks and bring something to Sarah to satiate her needs. I knew Johnson hated doing this as well. It was akin to a Mafia lord leaning on a shop owner for kickbacks. So, it would give him a reprieve.

I grabbed the cooler from the infirmary and headed out in one of the company cars, making a quick stop at my house to grab a secondary cooler. The agency didn't care what blood type was confiscated, but I did. I would only choose the most popular blood type because there was more of an abundance, but I also didn't want to take O negative, which could be used universally. So, my focus was on the O positive and the A positive, unless the bank was falling short on those; then I would take a few of the O negative. It made me feel slimy at best, but the blood banks seemed to be willing to part with enough bags to make it doable to fill my small cooler and still have a good amount in the agency's cooler for Manuel and the infirmary.

I dropped my cooler back at my place and headed to the agency to drop off the rest of the blood and the company car, exchanging it for my own. I headed home, grabbed the cooler, and then headed to Sarah's hoping this wouldn't be a mistake.

I paused at the door and took a breath, trying to get my mind set in the right place, but the way kissing her felt this morning kept clouding my mind and riling up my wolf. I knocked rapidly on the door, shifting my weight with the cooler in my hand. I certainly hoped this would help her fight whatever hunger she had to be feeling by now. I sent a text telling her I was here and inside, I heard her phone ping.

The door swung open, and a blast of sunshine hit her directly in the face. My heart slammed into my ribs, and I quickly stepped close, blocking the sun from hitting her. It took my brain a second to register.

She wasn't even singed by the sun. If she was a full-fledged vampire, that blast of sunshine would have blackened her face and left the stench of burning flesh on the air. I popped my mouth closed as she moved back and waved me inside. I stepped closer and reached out, running my thumb along the perfect skin of her cheek.

The only thing that had ignited was my libido. I wanted to slam her against the wall and kiss every inch of her skin. Instead, I whispered, "You didn't burn."

Her cheeks reddened. "No shit." Her gaze fell to the large cooler in my other hand. "What's that?"

I had almost forgotten the cooler. But in light of the last few minutes, I wasn't sure whether she needed it or not. "It...uh...may be a mistake." I cautiously placed the cooler in front of her and stepped back, putting space between us, as if the heat slithering inside me might actually turn into a blaze I couldn't stop.

She opened the top and stared before her gaze snapped to mine. "What did you do, steal these from a blood bank?"

I let out a nervous laugh. *If she only knew.*

"Jesus, Robby." She slammed the top closed and crossed her arms in that defiant way that reminded me of my mother when she was aggravated with my father.

"You need to eat." I shifted my weight as my own need increased. My wolf was restless and knocking at the cage again.

"Is this what you do for Manuel?" She turned a little green, and I looked away with a shrug.

The air around me changed, and I swallowed hard as my wolf nearly tore free. When I glanced back at Sarah, she was looking at me in a way that blew my resistance to shreds. And she was transmitting it through the air like a mating call in the wild.

"What are you doing?" My wolf's teeth came out. I trembled against his demands and stared at Sarah's amused gaze.

"I'm not doing anything. Why?"

"Because you are tossing out pheromones like dice at a craps table."

God, her gaze felt like a caress as it slid down my body. It was as if she were really seeing me for the first time in years. My pants became constricting against my hard member. *She doesn't understand what losing control means.*

She chuckled and sucked her lower lip between her teeth, slowly raking it as she released it.

"Please, stop," I pleaded. But those pheromones just increased, as if my plea turned her on. Her gaze went lower on my body, and I swear her eyes sparkled at the sight of my desire on display.

That broke me.

"Ah, fuck," I growled. The next thing I knew, I had her pinned to the wall again, but this time, instead of kicking me in the balls, she wrapped her legs around my waist, pulling me against her with the same kind of need accosting me. I searched her brown eyes for a moment. "What are you?" I whispered, but didn't wait for an answer. Instead, my lips descended onto hers with an eternal claim.

This was what my wolf wanted since the day I first saw her. This was what I had denied for fifteen years. This was what I wanted every day for the rest of our lives.

Futures be damned, I was claiming this woman, and nothing on God's green earth was going to stop me. I pressed my hips into hers, and she moved with the motion. Tearing at her clothing, I moaned in her mouth at the sweetness of her.

I forced myself up for air and moved my lips to her jawline, nipping at her skin, teasing her—and my wolf who insisted I claim her now. But I had made him wait fifteen years; I was going to enjoy every fucking inch of her before I claimed her.

She tugged at my shirt, and I moved my hands away from her, using the wall and my hips to keep her in place as I raised my arms. She peeled the T-shirt off me and tossed it aside. Her gaze landed on my throat and a flare of hunger crossed over her eyes before they met mine.

I paused and my breath kept coming in short bursts as I barely contained my wolf. "I'm supposed to be the alpha." I ground my hardness into her in a slow twirl of my hips. "I'm *supposed* to be able to control my wolf."

Her lips twitched into such an evil smile. "Maybe I don't want you to control your wolf. Maybe I want your wolf to ravage me."

Oh, fuck me. She knew just what to say to unleash him. "You have a wicked, wicked heart," I growled and wrapped my arms around her, carrying her to the living room couch.

Too many clothes. I tore what was left of her shirt off and tasted her skin, traveling lower as my member throbbed in my pants and my wolf nearly howled at the need stirring in my belly. I was going to make this a thousand times better than any of my wet dreams.

I nearly creamed my jeans at the thought as I took her breasts in my mouth, one after the other, rolling my tongue over her sensitive nipples. She arched into me and ran her fingers through my hair, whispering my name with such reverence.

I got her jeans unbuttoned and yanked them off her, moving my kisses down her belly while I situated myself between her open legs. The invitation in her eyes was just as much of an elixir as her citrusy scent.

I sucked on the inside of her thigh without losing eye contact with her. "I've dreamed of doing this for years," I admitted. Then I lowered my mouth to her sweet core. And God help me, I couldn't stop licking and teasing her. Not with the way she moaned my name. She was so fucking wet when I finally got my pants off. And she was panting as though I had taken her all the way to heaven.

I was so hard, and my wolf demanded I take her. I pulled away from the sweetness of her pussy, picked her up off the couch and put her on her knees in front of me; then I was inside her in one thrust. I closed my eyes, giving into the carnal need.

She arched into me, her shoulders leaned into my chest. Her breasts bounced with the force of my thrusts. I cupped one breast with my hand, twirling the hard nipple between my fingers as my other hand found her swollen clit and circled it slowly, knowing the dichotomy of movement would bring her over that brink again.

"Wicked woman," I breathed against her neck, playing her, holding on to my own release as it built. Her pussy clenched around me with her next orgasm, milking me, stripping me of any control.

I bit down on her shoulder, piercing her skin with my canines, claiming her as my passion blinded me. She screamed my name and clenched me again and again, as if marking her sent her into a giant wave of simultaneous orgasms.

Her blood coated my mouth, and I pulled my teeth from her as the connection solidified inside me. Her heart pounded in time with my own. Her hips moved just as violently as mine, and then I let out something between a howl and a moan in her name. My release was more like a fifteen-year pent-up explosion, infinitely more intense than anything I had experienced in my life.

I leaned forward so we both were half on and half off the couch. My breath panted in her ear as the fire of her soul blended with mine. A sense of lost time gripped me. I could have had this sensation that first night I met her if I had followed through on my wolf's demands.

I kissed the wounds I made. Wounds that would turn into my personal tattoo of claim on her. The bites would heal, but my mark would never fade.

She turned her head and stared at me. "You marked me."

I traced the cuts with my fingers, staining them with her blood. She was mine now and the MDA would have to understand. They'd have to back off. *Wouldn't they?*

I nodded before I met her incredulous gaze. She didn't look pissed like I expected. After all, I had just claimed her without her consent. "Yes."

I didn't have to hide my desire any longer. I also didn't have to hide the awe she inspired in me, or the love that had built over the last fifteen years. She was my sun. My moon. My everything.

And I would slaughter anyone who tried to take her from me.

The End

Continue Sarah and Robby's story with WICKED HEART - Book 1 of the Shades of Night Series.

About J.E. Taylor

J.E. Taylor is a USA Today bestselling author, a publisher, an editor, a manuscript formatter, a mother, a wife, a business analyst, and a Supernatural fangirl, not necessarily in that order. She first sat down to seriously write in February of 2007 after her daughter asked:

"Mom, if you could do anything, what would you do?"

From that moment on, she hasn't looked back.

In addition to being co-owner of Novel Concept Publishing, Ms. Taylor also moonlights as a Senior Editor of Allegory E-zine, an online venue for Science Fiction, Fantasy and Horror, and co-host of the popular YouTube talk show Spilling Ink.

She lives in New Hampshire with her husband and during the summer months enjoys her weekends on the shore in southern Maine.

Visit her at www.jetaylor75.com to check out her other titles.

WICKED HEART

Waking up to blood smeared walls certainly does not instill calm. Quite the opposite, considering I had locked my house up tight with deadbolts, sigils, and safety spells to ward away evil.

And I went to bed alone.

With no memory of a struggle and no signs of a dead body, there's only one logical conclusion. One of the demons we hunt at The Monster Defense Agency broke into my home.

My insatiable cravings clue me into exactly what I'm dealing with, and now I need to track the bastard down and fillet his ass.

Otherwise, my life will be forfeited, and I will become the hunted.

CROOKED SOUL

Escaping from captivity brings its own special challenges. Like dealing with PTSD along with major trust issues.

When an ancient vampire arrives from overseas, she comes with baggage from a past long before I was born. And she is hellbent on revenge.

Not only are we trying to dodge the monsters, but we are back on the radar of The Monster Defense Agency, and they are pissed.

If Robby and I can't get our shit together, either the MDA, or the master of the vampire that nearly destroyed us will finish the job.

TAINTED MIND

No one in the agency is safe from our wrath.

I am the last of my kind, deemed a monster by the Monster Defense Agency. But the MDA does not understand the hell their duplicity has unleashed.

Robby and I are now on our own hunting expedition.

Our target: the head of the MDA.

Although, it isn't just one man pulling the strings. It's a highly complex network that is more like a damn hydra. When you extinguish one, another pops out of the woodwork.

Two against an ancient organization that trains monster-killers and that knows all our tricks is even harder than it sounds. It's going to take all our skill and intelligence to kill this beast.

And being caught is not an option.

Other titles by J.E. Taylor that may interest you:

SEASON OF THE DRAGON TRILOGY

Monsters, trust issues, betrayal, and a near death experience.

What else could go wrong?

The end of life as we knew it didn't come with a nuclear blast. It didn't come with the deadly impact of a hurdling asteroid. No. It came in a wave of illness that swept the world with fear, and in our quarantined silence, the monsters awoke.

Leviathans, serpent kings, and dragons came forth from the bowels of the Earth. The season of the dragon began with fire and fury and ended with a new world order. One in which these giant terrorists held all the power.

When Mikhail St. Clare betrays the monsters by saving me from death at their claws, I cannot trust the last remaining dragon shifter. Not when humankinds' survival is at stake, and he had a hand in our near extinction.

The only thing we seem to agree on is our desire to annihilate the leviathans and unseat the Serpent King. Our personal futures depend on ridding the earth of these murderous overlords.

We thought crossing the leviathan-patrolled city where every corner hides a hideous death was our most lethal hurdle. But building a bomb large enough to wipe out an entire species carries its own insane levels of danger.

One wrong move and we could destroy everyone living in New York instead.

Find these titles and more on J.E. Taylor's website: www.JETaylor75.com!